William W. Hunter

The old Missionary

William W. Hunter

The old Missionary

ISBN/EAN: 9783743333734

Manufactured in Europe, USA, Canada, Australia, Japa

Cover: Foto ©Andreas Hilbeck / pixelio.de

Manufactured and distributed by brebook publishing software
(www.brebook.com)

William W. Hunter

The old Missionary

THE LIEUTENANT-GOVERNOR'S CAMP

The Old Missionary

By SIR WILLIAM W. HUNTER, K.C.S.I., M.A., LL.D.

TWENTY-THIRD THOUSAND

ILLUSTRATIONS BY MAJOR-GENERAL SIR CHARLES D'OYLY, BART.

HENRY FROWDE: 1897

Oxford

HORACE HART, PRINTER TO THE UNIVERSITY

CONTENTS

CHAPTER I.

CHAPTER II.

CHAPTER III.

CHAPTER IV.

ILLUSTRATIONS

———

THE OLD MISSIONARY

CHAPTER I

THE TWO ENCAMPMENTS

SUNDAY passed rather languidly in the Lieutenant-Governor's camp. The aide-de-camp had officially marked the claims of the day by appearing in his staff-spurs at breakfast, and the judge read service in the mess-tent. The small party then separated, the younger men to watch the cleaning of their guns and examine the scratches which the dogs had got during yesterday's jackal-hunt, the seniors to work off the arrears of the week or to write letters home.

It was only the flying camp of the Lieutenant-Governor of Bengal, and had little of the elaborate equipage which attends a progress of the Viceroy, or the prolonged cold-weather tours of the

Lieutenant-Governors of the North-west and the Punjab. Half a dozen tents on either side formed a short broad street down the middle of a mango-grove, with a strip of lawn between and a noble pipal-tree closing in the upper end. On the right of its towering masses of foliage stood the Lieutenant-Governor's pavilion, the British flag twisting lazily round its pole in the sunshine.

The tents of the Secretary to Government, the private secretary, the aide-de-camp, and the officer commanding the escort, were ranged in military line on one side of the lawn. The less regular row facing them was made up of the tents of our small District staff, the judge, the magistrate and his assistant, the superintendent of police, and the old doctor with his melancholy flute. A structure of yellow native cloth for mess purposes and public receptions stood at the head of our side of the little white street, and was connected with the Lieutenant-Governor's pavilion by a covered way of canvas across the grass. A few clerks, the troopers of the escort, and the servants, had their humble pent-roof encampment behind the pipal-tree on the outskirts of the grove.

After luncheon the party drew together again, and blue spires began to curl upwards from sociable cheroots under the tent door-flaps. The feathered republic of the grove also awakened from its noonday silence. The harmless December sun poured its floods of light through the foliage, carpeting the lawn with patterns of rich tracery. Two crows became suddenly aware that it was the afternoon, and fell to plotting in harsh caws how to steal their supper. A joint-family of minas, in their cold-weather plumage, resumed their lovers' quarrels where they had left off before their siesta, dashing from bough to bough in mock pursuit, amid much chattering and noisy flirtation. Squirrels with twitching tails and lizards with watchful glances ran up and down the trunk and lower arms of the great pipal-tree; a colony of little warblers fluttered in the middle stories; and one kite, wheeling on motionless wings above, kept a hungry eye upon all.

Presently the assistant magistrate, the aide-de-camp, and the escort officer rode off with the dogs, leaving their comrade the private secretary

to puzzle out the precedence of the hill chiefs who
were to attend the Darbar next morning. The
Secretary to Government, jaded by his day's
work, settled himself reposefully in a long cane
chair, with a glass of freshly mixed lemonade
and a volume of Browning. The judge came
forth from an interview in the pavilion; and it
fell to my duty, as magistrate of the District, to
attend the Lieutenant-Governor on his evening
ride.

Our path lay upward, across the dips and undu-
lations amid which the hill-country breaks down
upon the plains. The scrub jungle stretched
before us, until it merged in the heavier forest
of the mountains. On our left a broken line of
embankments came at intervals in sight, the remains of a road commenced as a relief work for
the highland people during a famine, and given
up when the scarcity passed off. Its grass-grown
sides, furrowed by four rainy seasons, and the
unbridged chasms left for the water-courses, were
eloquent with the silent reproaches of an unfinished work. I was pleading its cause, and urging
its completion as a means of opening up hill fairs;

throwing in the hope of a coal-mine on the route, from the argument of some rather unpromising shale which I had picked up in a gully.

'Ah! Ormiston,' said the Lieutenant-Governor, with good-natured pleasantry, 'so you too have joined the reformers! I thought that the work of the Secretariat might have rendered you a safe man. But I suppose you are now going to make up for three years of discouraging criticism of other men's projects by starting plenty of your own. Wherever I go it is the same. You Competition men come to Bengal with your heads full of ideas, and you expect me to find the money to carry them out. Why cannot you be content with things as you find them, as we were before you? It is only a few years since poor John Company was shovelled underground, and already his peaceful ways seem to belong to a remote antiquity.

'If I set down a man as a harmless sportsman, with his soul safely centred in his guns and dogs, he no sooner gets charge of a District than he sends up a report on the cattle disease, with a draft Bill for preserving the village pastures. If

he is a reading man, he has a scheme for rebuilding
our superfine education department on the rational
basis of the indigenous schools.   If law is his
fancy, he objects to the time-honoured practice of
the native magistrates taking evidence in two or
three cases at the same time, or he believes in the
possibility of reforming the Village Watch.   But
the District Officer with a taste for public works is
the most fatal of your gifted generation.   One man
wants to bridge a river, another to cut a canal, a
third dreams of cheap tramways.   Your neighbour
in the next District presented me yesterday with
a complete scheme for improved lock-ups, and you
yourself are manifestly in the early stage of road
fever.   I do not dare to take my Public Works
Secretary with me on tour, lest he should be won
over to your projects as well as myself.   But since
the Mutiny, the deluge!'

It was in the early time of promise, soon after
India had passed to the Crown, when the spirit
of improvement woke up from its long lethargy,
and each year brought forth some great measure.
The Codes which stand as stately landmarks at
the commencement of Her Majesty's rule were

recently enacted, and pledges that lay dormant during three-quarters of a century had been redeemed by the land-law defining the rights of the tillers of the soil. No one could have a better claim than Sir Charles Fairfax to a little comic grumbling at the rapidity of the pace, for no one in the old torpid days had been a stouter champion of progress. As his talk ran up and down the gamut from grave to gay, we insensibly wound into the hills. The scrub jungle gave place to fair-sized sál-trees; the couple of troopers who followed at a little distance were no longer visible, and only made their presence known by the crackling of their horses through the dry brushwood, or an occasional gleam of their lances among the foliage. Suddenly we came upon a scene in strange contrast with the secular thoughts and avocations of our own day. The forest opened out into a long grassy glade, in which the Old Missionary was holding his yearly gathering of the hillmen after the November harvest.

At the further end of the narrow valley a banian-tree rose in decaying dignity over a ruined shrine, which it had once climbed as a creeper. The

thin ancient bricks were clamped together in a
vegetable grasp stronger than iron, and the
domed roof now formed the heart of the mighty
stem.   The branches had thrown down suckers
to the ground, in which many of them had struck
and become new sources of sap, so that the pile
of foliage and timber was supported around its
magnificent circumference by colonnades of roots.
Two of these pillared recesses were converted into
huts.   An outer circle of hanging roots, with rude
structures peeping through, obscured the central
stem and ancient shrine.

In front of the wooded mass the Old Missionary
sat bare-headed on a steep bank of turf, with
a semicircle of elderly hillmen pleading some cause
before him.   To his right, half hidden among a
cloister of hanging roots, a fair little English
girl seemed to be explaining a picture-book to
a group of brown children.   Further off, on his
left, a crowd of hillmen and their wives squatted
around a native preacher who was haranguing
with earnest gesticulations.

It was one of the ancient halting-places on the
western pilgrim route, and had a story of its own.

THE MISSIONARY ENCAMPMENT

About four hundred years ago a Rajput chief and his wife rested here on their way to the holy city on the Orissa shore. The chief was childless, and having visited the shrines of the Upper Ganges in vain, he was at length wearied by the prayers of his princess into making the great pilgrimage to Jagannáth, from which few devotees then returned. His State lay near the desert in the north-west of India, eight months' march from the holy city on the Bay of Bengal. So he levied two years' taxes from his subjects; and having placed his territory in charge of his old Brahman Minister, he set forth with a train of nephews who might have given trouble in his absence, and a hundred of his bravest swordsmen.

After he and his princess, but more particularly the princess, had done everything that piety could suggest at the shrines of Benares and Gaya, they took the western route through the jungle to the Orissa coast. The chief, fatigued with so much unwonted religion, perhaps chose this route as only one more place of pilgrimage lay upon it, and his little band of Rajput chivalry made him careless of attacks by the forest tribes. His wife

no doubt learned with equal gladness that the
shrine on the way was one of those very ancient
retreats in which the wild worship of the hillmen
mingles with that of the Brahmans; shrines seldom
visited by reason of their remoteness, and therefore
the more efficacious in granting the prayers of
their devotees. The sport-loving chief hunted in
the forest with his followers as they journeyed
along. The princess performed her devotions
with her Spiritual Guide at every brook of flowing
water, and as they crossed each successive ridge
in the hills; halting for a full day's prayer whenever they came upon a spot where two streams met.

They had left behind them the shrine of the
hill-god, half temple half cave, with its weird rites,
and another month would bring them to the end
of their pilgrimage; to the abode of Jagannáth
on the Orissa shore. The gentle and beautiful
worship of Jagannáth, literally the Lord of the
Universe, before whom all men are equal, and
within whose purifying precincts alone all castes
can eat together, appeals in a special manner to
the repressed sympathies of Indian women. The
offerings to this much misrepresented god are

offerings of flowers and grain, not of blood.
Thousands of Hindus go through life with a longing
to partake of the consecrated rice at his shrine,
and to die at the 'Gate of Heaven,' a strip of sand
with the temple bells of his holy city on one side
and the boom of the ocean on the other. He is
the hearer of prayer; and the poor princess, like
many a childless woman since, was hastening the
march in the belief that she had only to pour out
her heart before the kind god, in order that its
desire should be satisfied.

But one evening the chief, who had been hunting
in the forest, was brought into camp clawed by
a bear. He died next morning, and the nephews,
having no leisure to settle their claims to the
succession, proclaimed the princess regent to give
them time for intrigue. She sent word that she
had already devoted herself as Sati, literally the
True Wife, and would rejoin her husband on
the funeral pile. The kinsmen tried to imprison
her by pegging down the door-flaps of the tent,
but the Rajput princess cut through the canvas
with her husband's sword, and calling down the
wrath of God on any who should stay her path,

she walked unveiled to the pyre and consummated
the awful rite. She had found her Gate of
Heaven—though not on the Orissa shore.

The nephews erected one of those little plat-
forms of brick, with a stunted dome and the rudely
carved impression of a hand, which at that period
marked the site of a Sati; burned down a space
in the jungle around it; and after the due rites
hurried north to fight for the succession. The
superstition of the hillmen kept the ground clear
in after generations. The grazing of the pack-
bullocks that halted there enlarged it, and a creeper
of the Indian fig or banian, which found root
in the crumbling monument, grew into a great
tree. The shape of the brick dome could still
be traced in the heart of its mighty hollow trunk.

The spot became a place for tribal meetings
of the hillmen, and a favourite camping-ground
on the western pilgrim route. One of the last
of the independent sovereigns of Bengal, having
happened to halt there with his troops, caused an
artificial lake to be dug for the use of travellers.
The tree, now about three hundred years old, still
went by the name of the Rajput Princess's Banian,

and a slab of blue-stone on the steps leading down to the water bore the Persian inscription of the Muhammadan king: 'By order of God, whosoever shall do a good deed, he shall be rewarded tenfold. Allah-ud-din, commonly called Husain Shah Badshah, son of Sayyid Ashraf Husain, constructed this lake. On him blessings. May God preserve his kingdom and his people. A.H. 922' (=A.D. 1516).

As we dismounted, the Old Missionary rose and courteously greeted his unexpected visitors. He was a striking figure, tall and gaunt, with a long white beard and large sunken eyes which had in them a look of settled calm. He and the Governor met as old friends, and after some talk between them about the past, Sir Charles begged our host to go on with the matter before him.

A hillman, who had been away from his village a few years at work on the new railway, loudly complained that, now he had come back, he found his homestead ploughed up, and his fields parcelled out among the tribesmen. The village head pleaded, in reply, the hill custom of re-distributing a man's land if he remained absent during two

C

harvests, but offered, according to that custom, to again allot to the returned kinsman a share in the hamlet fields, if he would give the usual feast to the village. 'But now that he has come back rich, he has grown stingy and will give nothing.' The other elders signified their assent to this unflattering statement, grunting out: 'He will give nothing; he will give nothing.' The complainant rejoined that the fields offered to him lay high, and beyond the reach of water from the village tank, while his old ones were among the best in the hamlet.

After hearing both sides the Old Missionary delivered judgement, that the man was to give a feast, that he was to get back a fair share of the watered lands with the grazing right for his buffa- loes in the jungle, and that, to make his name great, he should enlarge the village tank which no longer sufficed to irrigate the surrounding cultivation. The elders again signified their approval, repeating cordially: 'His name will be great; his name will be great.' The man also agreed, and the reconciled kindred moved off to have a friendly wrangle as to the exact outlay on goat-flesh and rice-beer.

Other village groups edged forward in front of the Missionary, with salutations of 'O Incarnation of Justice,' 'O Refuge of the Poor,' each bringing a boundary dispute, or a feud about the water-courses, or some knotty question of inheritance, which must otherwise be determined by blows. I afterwards learned that it was a practice of the Old Missionary on Sunday evenings in camp to settle all quarrels in the neighbouring hamlets, so that at least upon one day in the week the sun should go down on no man's wrath. Sir Charles, who remembered his friend's custom, sat down on the grassy bank beside him to watch the proceedings. My own attention was drawn to the throng around the native pastor, and thither I strolled, leaving the Old Missionary judging his little Israel under the tree.

The preacher, a young Brahman whose slender form and finely-cut features contrasted with the square-set bodies and bullet-heads of the hillmen before him, appeared to be coming to the end of his discourse. From the frequent recurrence of the words, I gathered that he was enforcing the text, 'Heaven and earth shall pass away, but My words

shall not pass away.' He spoke of the ancient hill
shrines in the country around, and how their poor
aboriginal gods had had to give place to the strong
clever deities from the Hindu plains. He reminded
the tribesmen that one Hindu priest after another
had come into their glens, each bringing his own
divinity, and each demanding separate offerings
under penalty of heaven-sent destruction and wrath.
There was a new Hindu god to be appeased at seed-
time, another to be paid at harvest, a third to be
propitiated in seasons of famine, a fourth for a con-
sideration would avert the small-pox, besides a multitude of lesser deities who took toll and tax at every
incident of domestic life. Here some accidental
listeners from a non-Christian hamlet muttered feel-
ingly, ' The Brahman speaks true.' So, he continued, your fathers were in bondage to many gods,
for there was no single one in whom they could put
their whole trust. Then he burst forth in praise
of the one Christian God, whose ear is open in all
seasons of sorrow and in all time of gladness: He
who slumbers not nor sleeps, but stands watch over
His people, as the mountains stood around their
homes, the same yesterday, to-day, and for ever.

I afterwards knew that Indian preacher well;
knew him when his higher nature seemed stifled
amid the paltry adulation of London drawing-
rooms; knew him also years later, when, in sorrow and solitude, he began afresh the work which
has endeared his memory to the hill races. But
never during the checkered years of his too short
life, neither at the height of his fame, nor in the
pathos of his self-abasement, can I recall anything
that came from him more impressive than the
words with which, then a youth fresh from college,
he ended his discourse in that forest glade. It
is difficult in a translation to preserve the effect,
at once simple and solemn, of his sentences as
they flowed forth in the native tongue:—

'Heaven and earth shall pass away. During
the first half of the harvest moon you see thousands of lights shooting through the air. You
call them the Reapers' Torches, and learned
men in cities say they are the materials of stars
rushing red-hot through the sky till they scatter
and go out. You think they come to tell you
when to cut your November rice. But God
sends them as His blazing heralds from heaven

to proclaim that the heavens themselves are passing away.

'Earth, too, is crumbling beneath our feet. The river from your hills no sooner spreads itself upon the low country than it begins to rend away its banks, tearing out for itself deep chasms every rainy season, and covering with water what was solid land. The villagers along its sides, as they listen in terror through the night to the thud, thud of the bank falling into the current, hear in every noise a warning that the river is drawing nearer to devour their homes. But those sounds are the voice of God sent forth from the darkness, declaring that this earth itself is passing away.

'Next harvest, when you lie out in the fields and see the Reapers' Torches in the air, say to yourselves, The heavens are telling of the glory of God; one night certifieth another. When you are floating down your sál-trees in the rains, and you tremble as the raft is swept towards the falling bank, say, The earth is the Lord's; He is my help and my deliverer; blessed be the name of the Lord. For who is God save the Lord, or

who is a rock save our God? Amid all changes,
He changes not. Heaven and earth shall pass
away, but one jot or one tittle of His word shall
not pass away until all be fulfilled. Amen and
amen.'

The short Indian twilight began to fade, and
it was time to return to our camp. The litigants
under the banian-tree had already dispersed, and
the Governor seemed to be arguing on some not
altogether harmonious subject with the Missionary, whose daughter, a sweet and silent child of
nine, was now nestling close to the old man's
side. Sir Charles jumped up as I approached,
and saying, 'At any rate, I shall think over it,'
rode off with a cordial farewell. For the first
few miles his pace left no leisure for any reflection
except how to keep one's head clear of the
branches. But as we emerged from the brushwood on to the hard fissured downs, he slackened
into a trot, and asked what I thought of the
young preacher. I said he was a man of remark-
able eloquence.

'I am glad to hear it,' replied Sir Charles, 'for
he is the first convert that my old friend has

ever felt sure of. In former days, if I ventured
to congratulate him on his success among the
people, he used to say, sadly, that during his long
life he had baptized many, but he did not know
that he had made a single Christian. Christianity,
he maintained, can only grow up among native
converts in the second generation. This Brahman
lad, whom he sheltered from the wrath of his rela-
tives and sent to college in Calcutta, has given the
Old Missionary a new hopefulness in his work.'

'But,' I interposed, 'who is the Old Missionary?
He has been out on his cold-weather tour ever
since I came to the District.'

'Not been long enough in the District to know
the Old Missionary, and yet long enough to
almost persuade me to double your budget allow-
ance for roads! Behold the ways of the Under-
Secretary turned magistrate. At any rate, I should
know him well, for I spent the happiest years of
my life within sight of his deserted house on the
Solway. The first sound that I seem to remember is the tramp of his father's wooden leg, as
the old Commodore stumped up the aisle of our
Cumberland village church. The Old Missionary

himself joined the fleet as a midshipman during its long watch outside Toulon, and saw Nelson's signal run up at Trafalgar. He left the navy at the close of the war, and after several wild years ending in a love-sorrow, he cut himself off from his former life and shocked his people by going out to India as a missionary. He had once, I believe, a sort of connexion with some Society, and received ordination from the Bishop of Calcutta; but he would take no pay, buried himself in the wilds of this then jungly district, and built his church and school-house at his own expense.

'When I was here as magistrate, he lived entirely among the natives, and one of his fancies was never to travel by carriage or horseback on an earth over which his Master had journeyed on foot. Trafalgar Douglas we used to call him, and already even his nickname seems to be forgotten! He has a child now, but I could as soon have imagined Saint Simeon Stylites a married man. The fact is that about ten years ago, a brother missionary on his way down from Benares died after a long illness in his house, leaving a daughter penniless and without a friend.

So Trafalgar Douglas, who was the soul of chivalry
to women although he never spoke to them, finding
it inconvenient to shelter the young lady on other
terms, married her. She died in giving birth to
the little girl whom you saw this evening.'

We rode on in silence, the Governor apparently
pursuing some train of thought which it was not
my place to interrupt. As our camp fires came
in sight, he suddenly asked :—

'How many of the hillmen have you still in
jail for their last outbreak ?'

'About fifty, sir,' I replied.

'Seven years,' he said, 'are a long time to have
suffered for a folly which was perhaps as much
our fault as theirs. The judge was at me all the
afternoon on their behalf; and strangely enough
the Missionary got upon the same subject. I must
say for Trafalgar Douglas that if we had listened
to his warnings, the oppressions of the money-
lenders which drove the tribes to revolt would
have been looked into before the rising instead
of after it. He kept his own hillmen quiet, too,
through the business, and so broke up the common agreement which might have rendered the

affair more awkward than it proved. He mentioned that there were nearly a hundred sentenced; what has become of the balance?'

'The doctor tells me that the older men pined to death in their first year of confinement. A few have been liberated; these that remain seem happy enough, and raise vegetables for the whole Station as well as for the jail. They have an idea that they are to serve the Queen for fourteen years, and then go back in honour to their villages.'

'Well, send me the record of the case, please; with the names of the ten against whom least was proved. I scarcely understand how the Missionary led me into a subject which I have always avoided with him. But the highest piety seems to win its way as unconsciously as the finest tact. What a work he has done in those hills without ever knowing it! I once asked him, when I was magistrate of the District, to tell me his secret for managing six thousand borderers without a policeman or a case ever coming into court. He answered simply that they were Christians. Why, his encampment to-night is on the

very spot where the clans assembled yearly
after the November harvest, to hold their drunken
festival of the New Rice, and then to sally forth
on their cold-weather raid upon the lowlands.
If anything were to happen to my old friend,
I wonder what would become of his Civitas Dei
in the forest.'

Next day we all rode with His Honour to
the borders of our jurisdiction, where the officers
of the next District were waiting for him. With
the help of the clever pen of the assistant magistrate, I made what we flattered ourselves was an
unanswerable case for the release not of ten but
of twenty of the hill prisoners ; experience having
taught us that if a District Officer is to get an
inch from the Secretariat he must show cause for
an ell. In a couple of months a release arrived
from Government for fifteen of them, and as the
Old Missionary had come in from camp, I rode
over to his house to tell him the good news.

CHAPTER II

THE SCHOLAR AND HIS CHILD

THE Missionary's dwelling was a straggling one-storied bungalow, with the thick thatch projecting low over the veranda. Originally it must have consisted of two small rooms. Various artless additions, jutting out at angles to avoid the sun or to catch the breeze, recorded the changing needs of a long life, as the want of an office for the sale of books, or of a dispensary for the sick, or of chambers for his wife and child, arose. But the rough wooden pillars of the veranda were festooned with flowering creepers which gave a picturesque unity and a grateful sense of greenness to the whole. The cottage stood in an ample orchard of mangoes, guavas, custard-apples, and other fruit-bearing trees, planted by the Missionary's own hand in skilful rows to allow free passage for the wind.

A servant told me that his master would be

back presently from Morning Service, and I amused
myself till his return by straying about his library.
This room, large, bare, and coarsely matted,
with only a folding camp-table and a few cane
chairs and country-made bookshelves rising to the
whitewashed canvas ceiling, had the faint smell of
damp volumes and decaying binding which is the
true odour of literature in Bengal. It opened on a
little rose-garden that led down by dilapidated brick
steps to a fish-pond overgrown with water-lilies,
from whose depths had been excavated the clay
for the thick mud walls of the house, and for
the mission chapel half screened by trees on the
opposite bank.

The Old Missionary's library contained a nonde-
script and rather tattered collection of grammars
and lexicons of the Indian vernaculars, a few Sanskrit texts, translations of the Testament in various
Indian dialects, medical works, and a dusty shelf
of treatises of the Irvingite sect. The inner end
of the room was lined with a bookcase partitioned
into pigeon-holes, for the manuscript slips of the
dictionary of the hill-language on which the old
man had long been at work. In earlier life he

compiled a grammar of that hitherto unwritten speech. The dictionary was the labour of his age, and as its progress became slower with advancing years, the venerable scholar had grown almost querulously anxious about its completion. Of late the assistant magistrate, and the Sanskrit pandit who followed the fortunes of that young officer, had been helping as volunteers. In a corner of the room stood a redwood press filled with books of a very different sort—voyages and naval biographies of the last century, with bundles of faded letters and papers sent out to the Missionary from his deserted Scottish home, on his father's death.

These bundles afterwards passed into my hands, and from them I have learned what I know about my old friend's family and life. The branch of the Douglases of which he was the last male representative perched securely through the Border wars on their tower overlooking the Solway. But an unlucky ancestor followed King James to London in 1603, and was one of those foolish Scottish gentlemen who ruined themselves by vying with the richer English courtiers. His impoverished descendants lost place among the magnates of

their shire, and they were hated by the peasantry
for their Episcopalian faith, which was all that
the spendthrift knight brought back from the
South. Before the Jacobite rebellions in the next
century, the family had sold their land almost to
the mouth of the river on whose high bank their
castle stood. Seignorial claims to harbour dues
embroiled each succeeding head of the house with
the fishermen and the masters of salt-sloops. The
king's officers suspected the Tower not merely
of the venial offence of smuggling, but of graver
dealings with the Pretender at St. Germains.

Only once during two centuries did the race
produce a man of note. This was a devoted
Anglican priest, whose character stood out in
strange contrast to the wild and sullen stock from
which he sprang. Having resisted for conscience
sake the warnings of the Covenanting farmers,
he was driven across the Border with violence,
and ended as a canon of Carlisle. Among the Old
Missionary's books an early copy of Quarles's
Emblems in wooden boards bore a faded signa-
ture, 'Carolus Douglas, presb.,' with the comment
'Rabbled in 1689' in a later hand. A quaint

duodecimo of 1633, the first edition of George Herbert's *Temple*, had the words 'Saved from the Rabblement' on the title-page.

The Douglases of the Tower emerged like many another depressed Scottish family during Lord Bute's brief supremacy in 1762. The heir of the house entered the navy, and, having raised a ship's company among the Solway fishermen, advanced in his profession. Forty-two years he passed in the service, forty of them at sea, sometimes cruising for over twenty months without dropping anchor. He became one of the famous 'chasing captains' of the long war, and purchased back a stretch of the family moorland with his prize-money. He retired with a shattered leg as Commodore, sailing home to the Solway in a half-sinking frigate which he had captured from the Spaniards, and afterwards bought in for a trifle from the Admiralty. With its timbers and fine mahogany planks he rebuilt the old staircase of the Tower, so that every morning he might have the fierce pleasure of treading the enemy under foot. A gentle Cumberland girl, whom he married during a short interval on shore, did not live long.

Their only child, now the Old Missionary, was early sent to sea. A letter in his boyish hand just after Trafalgar, told the weather-beaten father how his ship, 'the *Royal Sovereign*, Rear-Admiral Collingwood, was the first to break the enemy's line by passing astern a Spanish three-decker and ahead of a Spanish eighty-four,' together with several curious episodes of the fight. The gallant little midshipman was sent adrift at the close of the war.

What brought him out to India as a missionary some years afterwards, whether remorse for a misadventure in which a friend lost his life as seems hinted, or a love-sorrow as was popularly supposed, does not appear in the papers. He once mentioned to me that it was while reading Captain Cook's Voyages the missionary idea occurred to him. A few years of Evangelism convinced him, however, that little was to be done by mere preaching. He went home, studied in Edinburgh for a degree in surgery, and after coming under the influence of Edward Irving, returned to India as a medical missionary, deeply imbued with the mysteries and symbolism of the Catholic Apostolic

Church. In later life he advanced beyond this phase. Long before I knew him he had become simply the spiritual and temporal leader of the hillmen. He remained a Scotch Episcopalian as his forefathers had been; but with no strong dogmas, and only a great daily desire to do the best for his people.

Presently I heard him walking round the fish-pond from the little chapel, in converse with the young Brahman preacher of the forest glade. When they came to the door, the youth made a deep obeisance to his senior, and passed on to the school-house.

'Ah!' said the Old Missionary, after I had told my news, 'Providence is very kind. All my life I have been doubting whether there was any fruit of my labour. And now, in my old age, God has sent that young man to touch the hearts of the people in a way that I never could. You, too, bring welcome tidings about the deliverance of these poor hillmen. Only think, Mr. Ormiston, that good Brahman youth has secretly saved up the scholarship stipend which he won at college, saved it by stinting his own food for three years,

and has had a bell cast for the chapel.   He was
just asking leave to put up a belfry in which to
place it.   But I wonder what keeps Mr. Ayton?
He and his pandit are usually here and at work
before I come in from prayers.'

Ayton was the assistant magistrate.   A Boden
Scholar and a Fellow of his college, he formed one
of the brilliant group whom the Indian Civil
Service, on its being thrown open to competition,
attracted from the Universities.   On that morning
I had sent him out to look at a bridge on a new
road ten miles off, where the contractors were
trying to scamp their work.   I explained his
absence to the Missionary, and asked, with some
hesitation, if I could be of any use in his place.
The old man courteously concealed his chagrin,
and accepted the offer.   Meanwhile the pandit
slipped into the room with a dignified saluta-
tion, and the Missionary's little daughter silently
took her seat at the writing-table by her father's
side.

It was the last stage in dictionary-making, and a
novel experience to me.   The Missionary, having
collected his list of words among the highlanders

of the border, was not always certain whether they really belonged to the aboriginal hill-language, or whether they might not have been imported from the Sanskrit dialects of the plains. The slips of paper, each containing a word and its meanings, were brought forth from their alphabetical pigeon-holes and placed before him. The pandit, who sat contemplative, pronounced according to his ancient rules whether each successive word had a connexion with any Sanskrit root. Meanwhile I examined the lexicons of several Indian vernaculars, to see if it had a counterpart in the dialects of the lowlands. When the process was finished and the result noted down, the little daughter neatly pasted the slip in its alphabetical order on a sheet of tough yellow country paper—yellow from the arsenic which had been mixed in the pulp to protect it from fish-insects and white ants.

It required a more profound knowledge ot Sanskrit than I possessed, although in my time a High Proficiency man, to check the learned pandit's decisions. In fact, my only use was to save the · Missionary's eyes, which had lately been troubling

him, by looking through the dictionaries of the
lowland dialects. The old man felt the want of
Ayton's finer touch; and I was glad when, soon
after eight, the short springy canter of an Arab
along the road announced his approach.

'Quick, May dear,' said the Missionary. 'Get
some tea and toast. I hear Mr. Ayton's horse,
and he must have been out before sunrise.' Presently that gentleman appeared in boots and spurs,
a tall and handsome young Yorkshireman, rather
heavy for the high-bred animal he rode.

'It was good of you to come so quickly,' was
the old man's welcome. 'We have still two hours
before breakfast. But the roads are like iron now,
and I hope you have not ridden your Arab too
hard.'

'Not a bit, thank you,' replied Ayton; 'I sent
a pony on halfway, and Amir is all the better
for having a little taken out of him these cold
mornings.'

So we went to work in earnest, Ayton agreeing
with the pandit and passing each word in a
moment, or disagreeing with him, and flashing the
light of Western philology on the Brahman's old-

world methods. In either case his decision gave
that sense of finality which had been wanting before. But the quicker we got through the little
pile of slips, the more nervous the old scholar became to hasten the pace. He seemed to feel, too,
that every word which Ayton rejected as not really
belonging to the hill-language was a personal loss.
Once or twice, when several had been thus put
aside in succession, a troubled look passed over his
face. At such moments the silent little girl would
touch his elbow almost imperceptibly with her soft
cheek, and the old man, without seeming to per-
ceive the motion, at once resumed his air of habitual
gentleness. Shortly after ten we broke up, Ayton
and I galloping home to bathe and breakfast before
going to our respective Courts.

A few weeks afterwards, in passing the Missionary's cottage, I saw a bullock-cart under his trees,
and that small bustle of baggage-carriers and servants about the veranda which in India betokens a
move into camp. I rode up to ask what could be
taking my old friend out so late in the season, with
the hot winds of April already blowing. He was
sitting at his writing-table, with the dictionary un-

heeded before him, much perturbed by news of a riot attended by bloodshed in a Christian village forty miles off. I found the place lay in the direction of a jungle tract where I had to settle certain forest disputes—a part of my cold-weather tour which I reserved till the drying up of the higher water-courses might give me a chance at a tiger during my visit. I begged the old scholar to allow me to drive him out, and said I could arrange to start next morning. At first he declined, explaining that only his infirmities and his unwillingness to leave his child at home, with no English lady in the station, had led him to use a conveyance at all. His objections to driving, whatever they may once have been, were of no sentimental sort. Experience taught him, he said, that it was only by walking with a few disciples from hamlet to hamlet that he had in early years been able to win the confidence of the villagers, and he was afraid of impairing his influence in his old age by coming among them in any less simple form.

I suspect he was right. Indeed it often occurred to me that we officials, by our horses and retinues of well-dressed servants, always give

the natives a fear that they are intruding—a
fear which only the greatest administrators like
Lawrence and Malcolm, and the greatest mission-
aries like Carey and Duff, have quite overcome.
I urged, however, the waste of half a week away
from his beloved dictionary in doing by bullocks
what horses could accomplish in a half-dozen hours.
The risks to his little girl from several days' ex-
posure so late in the season in a country cart, with
only a thin covering from the sun, were also con-
siderable. In the end he allowed himself to be
persuaded; so my tents went off in the afternoon,
and next morning we started at daybreak.

At that time I used on my District tours, when
not riding, a light strong Stanhope which I had
bought during a three months' holiday in Australia,
broad enough to go down the steep banks of the
gullies without overturning. Its width allowed the
little girl to sit between the old man and myself on
the front seat, and it was pretty to see how the shy
child grew into a bright and observant companion.
During the first ten miles she watched the horses
working, without a word. When we paused at the
end of the stage for our second pair, and to have

coffee under a tree, her small motherly cares for her father were very pathetic.

Not less touching were her surprise and delight at the modest preparations which had been made for her comfort on our next halt, during the heat of the day. It was one of the ordinary wayside mango-groves used for camping by the District officers on tour. But the trees were in full flower, and my people, with the native's natural politeness, had tried to make her little tent pretty. Her exclamations of pleasure at finding her old nurse, who had come on an hour earlier in my dog-cart, and her little zinc bath, with her fancy work-basket and a story-book and some flowers on a miniature wicker-table, 'just as if she was at home,' spoke of a childhood passed in ignorance of those petty attentions which are a matter of course to English children in India.

All forenoon the servants, proud of their un- wonted charge but rather anxious, were trotting after her with a sun-umbrella as she popped in and out of the two tents, in the shade of the thick green foliage. Now it was the first relay of horses march- ing into the grove, and she must go forth to see them fed. Then it was the second pair being sent off to wait for us on the road, and she must give them a parting plateful of chopped sugar-cane. Her innumerable discoveries among the blossom-laden trees, about the squirrels, and the flashing scolding jays, and the very human antics of the long-tailed monkeys, and a harmless water-snake who had landed from a neighbouring pond to warm himself in the spring sunshine, were poured forth every few moments as she rushed into the tent where her father reposed. The old man forgot his unfinished work at home, and the trouble-some task awaiting him on the morrow, and listened to her swift succession of news from outside with a pleasure scarcely less childlike than her own. After luncheon she read him to sleep, and then plied her fingers silently over some small feminine industry, watching his slightest movement. It was the broken sleep of anxious old age. If he started or muttered, she at once went on reading at the point where she had left off, and the uneasy dreamer without open-ing his eyes became calm at the sound of her voice.

When at length he awoke, her quick little divinations of his wants, and the way in which

she gently but effectively **took** charge of our
comforts, were very sweet. One might have supposed that she had all her life been accustomed
to make afternoon tea for two gentlemen under
the door-flap of a tent.

On our third stage of ten miles in the cool
of the evening, she became such a friend of the
horses that she held the reins. Before the fourth
stage was over, her little head, wearied out with
the excitement of the long day, was sound asleep
on her father's shoulder. As we splashed through
the river, beyond which shone the windows of the
Factory where we were to rest for the night, she
opened her eyes wonderingly on the shallow line of
water silvered over by the moonlight. Then mur-
muring 'How beautiful,' she nestled closer to her
father and fell over again in a moment. Presently
the horses were straining up the high river-bank,
and we carried her wrapped in a shawl, but still
fast asleep amid the red glare of torches and the
hearty greetings of our host, into the ancient
Factory.

THE ANCIENT FACTORY

CHAPTER III

THE PARTING OF THE PEOPLE

THE Factory, once a residence of the native Viceroys, was perched upon the steep river-bank. Massive buttresses had protected its many-angled walls and bastions against the current until fifty years ago, when the channel shifted across to the opposite side of its broad bed, leaving their solid foundations high and dry in the air. During the rainy season the floods still dashed against the outworks. But throughout eight months of the year, one looked down from the battlements on a distant thread of water glistening amid a wide expanse of sand.

It was one of the East India Company's earliest silk factories in Bengal, planted on the edge of a forest region which had yielded the delicate fabrics worn in the Imperial seraglio. Fortified alike against the river and the hill tribes, it be-

came a safe place for merchandise and industry
during the breaking up of the Mughal dynasty.
Settlements of silk-weavers clustered under its
walls, and the surrounding jungle was gradually
thrust back before an advancing semicircle of
mulberry cultivation. When the East India Company retired from trade to concentrate its energies
on government, the old Factory and its adjacent
lands were bought for a small price by an
Italian. This worthy artisan had been brought
out to instruct the Company's silk-workers in
better methods of treating the cocoons, and, after
faithful service to his Honourable Masters, found
himself in his old age making a fortune for himself. His first thought was to obtain the companionship of a fellow-countryman in his exile,
and at the same time to render thanks to our
Lady of Siena for his good luck. He accomplished both objects by sending for his nephew, one
of those kindly peasants dipped in ink who then
formed the rank and file of the Italian priesthood.

The young kinsman proved to be a man with
plenty of rustic shrewdness, and he made himself
quite at home among the husbandmen. Indeed,

the Indian peasant proprietors were exactly of the class amid whom he had been born and brought up in Tuscany. He won their goodwill by stamping out a troublesome disease of the silk-worms, partly by improved ventilation, but visibly aided by the sprinkling of holy-water in the breeding sheds, and by a procession through the mulberry fields, himself marching at its head with the Host and a censer, lustily chanting a Latin psalm.

The simple folk saw no harm in adding the pretty stucco Lady, whom he set up in an outhouse, to the other deities that they propitiated at various stages of the cultivation. On the death of his uncle the whole concern came under his pastoral sway. His people willingly paid him the little compliment of bringing their babies to be baptized, the more gladly as he tied a small silver coin round the neck of each infant Christian. He attempted no flights in orthodoxy, but was quietly happy to see, on the annual festivals of the Church, an increasing throng of devotees arrayed in their holiday garments, streaming in from the hamlets to lay their rosemary garlands before his tinsel shrine.

He in his turn passed away at a ripe age, and the Calcutta firm who next bought the Factory found to their surprise that they had a Christian population on their hands. The Scottish gentleman at the head of the business engaged an elderly disciple from the Serampur Mission to look after the villagers, and, having thus satisfied his conscience, troubled himself no further in the matter. The elderly disciple settled down in sleek and friendly comfort among his isolated flock: his Baptist theology but little interfering with the careless Romanism left behind by the Italian priest.

When the Company of Jesus assumed active charge of the Catholic communities in Lower Bengal, they sent an agent to report on this lapsed settlement. Their missioner found the villagers in contented enjoyment of a union of Christian and Hindu rites, of proved efficacy for bringing seasonable rain, for preventing blight among the silk-worms, and for propitiating the many local deities who concern themselves with the mulberry cultivation. The chief sign of their Catholic faith was the firing of the three old

Factory cannon, named the Father, the Mother, and the Son, on Easter morning and Trinity Sunday. The acute Jesuit also thought he detected a relic of apostolic teaching in a sort of spell used over the sick when administering medicine, *Patan Noshtan Keshan Shelas*—apparently a diversion for pathological purposes of the *Pater noster qui es in cœlis*, as pronounced by the Italian peasant-priest.

By one of those seeming misapplications of force which occur from time to time in the history of the Jesuit Missions, a man of high culture was sent to revive the faith in the little silk-weaving settlement. After earning fame as a mathematical professor in the seminaries of the Order in Belgium and at Rome, Father Jerome had been brought out to India to fill a similar post in Saint Xavier's College at Calcutta. Whether as a discipline in humility, or as a period of sequestered self-preparation for the great office afterwards laid upon him, or for what other reason I know not, he was suddenly deputed to the petty colony of jungle Christians on the river-bank. But if the Company of Jesus sometimes appears

E

to the careless onlooker to misdirect force, its
sons seldom fail to justify its action.   In six years
Father Jerome changed the whole spiritual life of
that isolated community.

He had given shelter during a famine to a couple
of hundred orphans, baptizing them promptly,
and feeding them, educating them, and bringing
them up to husbandry or handicrafts, with the
help of the modest rupee a month which the
Government allowed per head for their main-
tenance.   By the labour of their willing boyish
hands he built a church.   The Factory granted
a plot of arid ground on the high river-bank :
one part of which he turned into a brickfield, while
the other served as a site.   The hill Raja, with
Hindu benevolence to religious men of whatever
faith, allowed as much timber from the forest as
was wanted for the rafters and porch.   At the
head of his juvenile band the Jesuit Father ex-
plored the torrent beds and gullies, and collected
a store of the nodular limestone which makes
such capital mortar.   In five years, unaided by
a single grown-up artisan, he had erected a church
of no mean proportions, with a Virgin in blue

and gold in the niche of the belfry, conspicuous for miles up and down the long river reach. The brickfield had been turned into the Priest's Tank, well stocked with fish, and yielding enough water to keep green a little graveyard.

But with his prosperity came sorrow. For the Scottish firm in Calcutta, scandalized at its villagers being turned again into Papists, sought the help of the Old Missionary of the District, and persuaded him to send a more active Protestant pastor to take charge of the strayed flock. 'Trafalgar' Douglas interfered unwillingly, for he privately believed that the change had been on the whole for good. But having consented, he gave his best man to the work—the young Brahman preacher whose eloquence had struck me at the missionary encampment in the forest glade.

For a time his fresh enthusiasm carried everything before it, and when the failing health of Mr. Douglas led to the youth's recall to headquarters, he left the weaving settlement on the river-bank divided into two religious parties. His successor, a native preacher of lower caste, quarrelled with the Jesuit priest. The result was a series of petty disturbances, ending in a bloody affray on Easter morning when both factions asserted with clubs and rusty spears their claim of priority to fire off the three old cannon.

On our first evening at the Factory the Catholic clergyman, as the only other European in the place, was duly invited to dinner. During our progress through the preserved salmon and tinned *entrées*, the gram-fed mutton, and the fattened turkey and Yorkshire ham, which the hospitable planter lavished on the long-drawn-out repast, Father Jerome attracted us by an extreme gentleness of manner, and by his varied and interesting talk. One felt in Europe again, notwithstanding the punka waving overhead. He gave the impression of a penetrating intelligence, but of a diffident nature—a self-contained observer who had come in contact with historical personages of our day, but who seemed stranded in middle life, a resigned and lonely man.

The little girl, who now emerged from her evening sleep, hungry and very wide awake, was quickly won by his half-shy friendliness and worn, delicate face. The Old Missionary

watched him with grave Scottish courtesy from
under his sagacious white eyebrows, but was too
tired at first to take part in the conversation.
After dinner the clergymen retired with their
cheroots to the veranda, where the child fell
fast asleep again on her father's shoulder, until
her nurse carried her off. The planter, perhaps
thinking that his reverend guests might learn
to know each other more easily without the
presence of third parties, engaged me in a game
of Nap. Somewhat to my surprise, the two
padres were still in deep converse in the moon-
lit veranda overhanging the river when I went
to bed.

Next morning the police inspector came to
me at daybreak, with his official entries of what
had been going on in the village during the
past month. They showed that things were worse
than I supposed, and that the religious affray
was the outcome of deeper causes of disturb-
ance. The truth is that the people had outgrown
the village lands. As long as the silk Factory
prospered, the high profits of the mulberry
cultivation kept them all in tolerable comfort.

But the keener competition of Italy and France
was beginning to tell on the silk production of
Bengal, and many of the mulberry fields had
been ploughed up for the less lucrative rice-crop.
The old families of the hamlet, who still clung
to their mulberry cultivation, were for the most
part Roman Catholics—the descendants of the
original weaving settlement in the days of the
East India Company.   The poorer rice-growers
were generally Protestants, and they bitterly
complained that the mulberry enclosures, on the
plea of the former village custom, monopolized
the water-supply of the hamlet.

Before the Easter riot over the three old guns,
there had been a dozen fights about cutting the
irrigation channels.   The planter, a keen sportsman and a capital fellow but withal a cautious
Edinburgh man, who represented the Calcutta
firm, had done his best to keep things quiet.
He prudently stood aloof, however, as soon as
the quarrel took a religious turn.

I was sitting in a puzzled mood, with the
police day-book and village map before me, when
the Missionary tapped on the open door and

asked if I could spare a few minutes. I gladly begged him to come in, as a man in perplexity welcomes any diversion which postpones the process of making up his mind. But instead of accepting the proffered chair, my old friend stood erect on the other side of the writing-table, and without preface said:—

'Mr. Ormiston, I am come to make a request. I communed long with Mr. Jerome last night, and I found him a righteous man. And this morning in my prayers the words were borne upon me: "Let there be no strife, I pray thee, between me and thee, and between my herdmen and thy herdmen; for we be brethren. Is not the whole land before thee? Separate thyself, I pray thee, from me. If thou wilt take the left hand, then I will go to the right; or if thou depart to the right hand, then I will go to the left." I ask you, Mr. Ormiston, not to deal with this matter, but to leave it to him and me.'

I felt rather sceptical about settling a case, clearly provided for by the Code of Criminal Procedure, on the basis of texts out of Genesis; so I replied:—

'But, Mr. Douglas, what if you cannot agree?'

'Then, sir, God's will be done. But I ask you to remember that for forty years my people have never been seen in the police courts, and I trust, with God's help, that they will not be seen there in my old age.'

I reflected for a minute, with a growing sense of the unlikelihood of his success but also with a growing respect and pity for the brave old man, before answering:—

'Very well, Mr. Douglas. I can take no cognizance of your private arrangements with Father Jerome; but I have some business in the hill-country, and I shall go away for three days. When I come back, if everything is settled, well and good. If not, I must do what seems needful.'

The Old Missionary bowed in silence, although his lips moved. I only realized by the trembling of his thin long fingers, which had unconsciously clasped the edge of the table, that an interview which was to me merely an ordinary matter of business, had been to him a great strain and a great relief.

I went out at once into the Factory enclosure,

where the villagers were sitting under trees waiting
to pay their respects to the newly arrived magistrate.   After the customary civilities, I told them
that I had heard of their misdeeds, and called on
each faction to point out five ringleaders on the
other side.   When the ten stood before me, and
I had learned from the police inspector that they
were really the chief disturbers, I briefly told
them that I was going for three days into the
hill-country, and on my return would listen to
their complaints on the spot.   Meanwhile, if any
affray took place, the police would march those
ten men, together with any others engaged, across
the District to be tried at my headquarters' Court.
Needless to say, they assured me that nothing
would happen to bring such shame on the village.
So with a doubtful mind, yet not without a half
hope that I had done a fair morning's work,
I came in out of the sun for a hasty bath before
breakfast at eleven o'clock.

During that ample meal, which the Bengal
planter knows how to augment into a high
function of his hospitable day, my host offered
to ride an afternoon's march with me into the

forest. Within an hour his trackers had started
to see if they could get news of game, and
a joyful *posse comitatus* of the low castes in the
village was assembling on the chance of sport
a score of miles off next morning. I sent on
a mounted orderly to warn the hill Raja that
I would reach his fort the following evening, to
look into the quarrel between him and his fief-
holders. We rode five-and-twenty miles in the cool
of the afternoon, slept a few hours under a tree,
and were lucky enough to cut off a tiger in a gully
on his way back from his drink before sunrise to
his higher retreats. Then we drew the jungle,
and the beaters returned home rejoicing in four
deer, a leopardess, and a motley bag of small
game. The planter galloped home to the Factory
in time for his midday breakfast, and I went on
with some of my people to the Raja's fort.

The business there easily arranged itself. The
planter, finding the silk Factory growing less pro-
fitable, had invented a trade in sál-wood sleepers
which he floated down the river to the railway
during the rains. The feud between the Raja
and his under-holders, although complicated by

armed encounters between their retainers and
by mutual reprisals in forest-burning, was really
a question of the fair division among them of
the new and unforeseen value of their woods.
As the tract lay on the Non-Regulation frontier
of the District and the disputants were simple
hill-chiefs, they had a long day's inconsequential
wrangle and, when well tired out, harmoniously
accepted my award. Their return to friendship
was celebrated by a big shoot in the jungle, with
much pomp of elephants in tinsel trappings and
of albino-eyed horses with pink tails, but too
noisy for serious sport. On the evening of the
third day I returned to the Factory.

'Glad to see you back,' said the planter, as
I dismounted. 'But you have missed a curious
sight. Since you left they have been holding
a sort of General Assembly of the Kirk, with the
villagers swarming about in their best clothes,
like the country ministers and elders on the Edinburgh Mound in the fourth week of May. The
upshot of it all was that either the Protestants
or the Catholics must hive off; but which were
to go? The Catholics had their mulberry gardens

and their new church; the Protestants had their
rice-fields and most of the village cattle. Father
Jerome came out strong. He got his people into
the church and kept them there till he worked
them up to the pitch of buying out the others.
The fat grain merchant brought a bag of rupees,
the mulberry-growers dug up their hordes of coin,
and the women threw their ornaments in a heap
before the altar. I had no idea there was such
a weight of bangles in the village. Then they
held a council of five, the padres sitting with them,
and valued the rice-growers' holdings. They were
at it pretty well for two days and two nights, and
this morning everything was settled, and the sealed
bags of silver were locked up for safe-keeping in
my treasury until your arrival.'

'How did Mr. Douglas manage to get the
Protestants to agree to move?'

'That old man is marvellous! Jerome's word
was law with his own people. But Douglas is
almost a stranger here, and when the Protestant
rice-growers saw their way to a good bargain they
stood out for higher terms. The women, too,
raised a lamentation at quitting their old homes,

where they have not had one full meal a day
during the last three years. Yesterday everything
seemed hopeless. But I never saw a man like
Mr. Douglas, for quietly putting down his will.
He seemed to speak with an authority they
dared not resist. I myself, when passing the
open door of their conventicle, felt half afraid
of the rigid old prophet, with his set face, and
white hair, and lean uplifted arm, as he stood
haranguing them.'

'Still, they were within their rights to refuse
to move.'

'That may be. All I know is, that by yesterday afternoon he had won the best of the Protestants to his views. They gradually showed the
rest what fools they would be to lose what is really
a very good chance. To the jungle herdsmen
with cattle but no holdings, and to the landless
labourers, Mr. Douglas promised a sum for each
family, enough to set up a hut and buy a plough.
I hope the old gentleman can afford it, for he
seems to have no ready cash, and has given me
a power of attorney to sell out his Government
paper in Calcutta. In the end the malcontents

had to give in—their breath fairly squeezed out
of them between the sensible people who were
satisfied with a fair offer, and the herdsmen and
landless families who saw their chance of bettering
themselves in life.'

'But where are they to get the land? It needs
a long purse to break up old forest.'

'That's true, and if they had to take in the
jungle on this side of the river, they would make
a poor thing of it. But we have three villages
on the western bank, within the old Factory grant,
which were demolished by wild elephants fifty
years ago. The elephants have disappeared off
the face of the earth since the road was made
through the hill-country. But as long as the
mulberries and silk-worms paid well, it was not
worth our while to resettle those outlying villages.
When the people had used up the pasture-lands
on this side of the river for growing rice, they
began to resort to the other bank for feeding
their buffaloes. The Factory took care however
to prevent any grazing rights accruing, so that
the land is still waiting to be settled for cultivation.
Now is my chance to re-people the deserted

villages, and of course the Factory gives the seed *gratis* for the first year, and the land during the next two years free of rent.'

'And how about the dispute and the three cannon?'

'Oh, that was the least part of the business. Luckily neither side had lodged a complaint, so the police need not take notice of a few broken heads which are now mended, unless they get orders to do so. Last night the two factions joined in a village feast of friendship and farewell. Poor Jerome, who has never had a rupee beyond his daily food since he came here, somehow produced two goats. Mr. Douglas asked me for a sheep, and the row and drum-beating went on to the small hours. This morning the headmen of both sides came and begged the old cannon from me. One, they set up as a pillar on this bank; another they have buried in the sand halfway across; and the third is to be posted on the opposite bank at the spot where the new village will be built. Some mat huts have already been put up, and Mr. Douglas started with his people an hour ago to mark out the land, so that

they may begin ploughing as soon as the first
rain comes.'

As he was speaking, we reached the veranda
looking down on the river. Father Jerome was
leaning over the balustrade at the further corner,
apparently too rapt in his own thoughts to observe
our arrival. Halfway across, a long line of men
and women and cattle were moving slowly westward
through the heavy sand: the tall form of the Old
Missionary in front, hand in hand with his little
girl. When they came to the shallow channel, we
saw a group run forward and try to raise him up,
in order to carry him over. But he refused, and
lifting his child in his arms, stepped into the
stream. As he reached the middle, the rays of
the setting sun flashed across the water to us,
throwing a glory around the grand gaunt figure
erect under its burden. The pilgrim band slowly
filed through what seemed a river of light.

When their feet touched the dry expanse of sand
on the other side, they raised the Evening Hymn
to a plaintive Bengali air. Then a little later the
whole multitude burst forth with the triumphant
thanksgiving of the Old Hundredth Psalm, as they

THE START FOR NEW HOMES

began to ascend the steep distant bank. We silently watched the last of them disappear under the jungle which fringed its high ridge, already fading into the night. On turning round I saw Father Jerome rising from his knees at the further end of the veranda. His eyes were filled with tears.

CHAPTER IV

THE GOING DOWN OF THE SUN

THAT hot weather was one of the hottest and happiest which I spent in India. It was my first year in independent charge of a District, with the endless interests of the position intensified by youth, and still unblunted by wont. It was passed too in close intimacy with a man marked out by his talents for a brilliant career, and by the sweetness of his nature for intimate and enduring friendship.

Arthur Ayliffe had held his treasury and jail in 1857 with eighty policemen and the half-dozen sporting rifles of his District staff against three successive bands of mutineers, each of whom outnumbered his little force tenfold. A Companionship of the Bath and quick promotion were his well-earned rewards. While still a young magistrate he found himself appointed Commissioner of the

six western Districts of the Lower Ganges, stretch-
ing from the swamps of the Hugli to the forests
and mountains which separate Bengal from the
Central Provinces. The population of this wide
tract amounted to about seven millions—a great
diversity of races, with the astute Hindu at the
one end and the primitive aboriginal tribes at
the other.

During several years Ayliffe won golden opinions
by calming down the excitement which a local
rising of the hill-people in 1855 had left behind.
But on the passing of the famous series of Codes,
the Calcutta Secretariat worked itself into a fervour for legal symmetry against which he set
his face. In one of his protests against applying
a uniform procedure to races in widely different
stages of human society, he was held to have gone
beyond the decorous limits of official remonstrance.
No public scandal followed. The too outspoken
Commissioner merely found it expedient to take
furlough. On his return he was gazetted to the
judgeship of the District in which I was then
serving--one of the six formerly in his charge.

He swallowed the pill in silence. In those days

a District judgeship, which is now rightly recognized as an important post demanding a special training and no mean capacity, was held in small esteem. The District judges were for the most part heavy elderly gentlemen, who had not made their mark in the more active branches of the administration. To this rule there were indeed brilliant exceptions. But generally speaking, the abler men regarded the office as an unavoidable halt in their promotion from Magistrate of a District to Commissioner of a Division; or as a *locus penitentiae* for a Commissioner who had had a difference with the Government, or made a mistake. In Ayliffe's case the Service felt some indignation, as the Government soon afterwards found itself constrained to relax the uniformity of the Codes to which he was sacrificed. But the sympathy of his brother officers fell flat, Ayliffe himself seeming quite content with the change. He went to work on his judicial duties as keenly as if he had given up any thought of higher advancement, save the humdrum promotion by seniority to the Supreme Court.

The judge's house was an imposing white edifice,

with Doric pillared verandas and a flat roof, in the
middle of an extensive park dotted with ancient
trees. A long avenue led across the parched sward
to the judge's garden, which was separated from
the main park by a public road. This garden, the
work of a line of judges during a hundred years,
was the one spot always green in our arid station.

In the good old days of John Company,
when the District officers freely used jail labour,
gangs of prisoners had excavated in the judge's
garden a broad winding piece of water which
expanded almost to the dignity of a lake. Its
cool depths and shady margin formed a rustic
swimming-bath of singular beauty. Artificial hol-
lows supplied moist beds for a luxuriance of gay
flowers, which were screened from the hot winds
by blossoming shrubs and forest trees. The mud
delved out for the lake eighty years ago had been
erected into a little hill, now clothed with an
orange-grove known as The Mount, and somewhat
suggesting the mound in New College garden
at Oxford. From the arbour on its summit one
looked across the undulating country to where
the sun set among the western hills. The further

end of the spacious garden was walled off for the station grave-yard—the first English grave having been dug for the little daughter of a judge at the end of the last century.

In our small station each officer had a house assigned to him by custom. The judge's house, the magistrate's house, and the assistant's bungalow, were from time immemorial rented by a succession of the officers whose names they bore. Indeed, they appear even in the survey maps under those unchangeable designations. My dwelling, the magistrate's house, had fallen into disrepair; and that year the landlord, on commencing the annual patching up, found the beams which supported the heavy flat roof completely tunnelled out by white ants. This meant four months in the hands of workmen, and the judge kindly offered me quarters during the slow process of re-roofing. It was not considered quite regular for the judge and magistrate to live together, as the executive and judicial powers in a District at that time often came into collision. But no one else had a house with sufficient spare room to take me in, so my hens and ducks and guinea-fowls were driven over to Ayliffe's poultry-yard, and I took up my abode with my friend.

It was altogether a bachelor station. Not one of the three civilians was a married man, the doctor was a widower, and the wife of the district super-intendent of police had gone to England with her children. The hot winds set in like a consuming fire. The large double doors which form the windows of an Anglo-Indian house stood open all night, and were shut up tight in the early morning; the heavy venetian frames outside the glass doors trying in vain to hermetically seal the interior from the glare and heat. We had to start for our gallop by 5 A.M., or not get it at all except at the risk of sunstroke. The public offices opened at seven, and closed for the day at noon. Then each man drove swiftly through the furnace of shimmering air to his darkened and silent home.

A lingering bath and a languid breakfast brought the hot hours to one o'clock. The slow combustion of the suffocating afternoon was endured somehow under the punka, with the help of the endless bundles of papers in one's office-box, read by chance rays which fiercely forced an entrance

through every chink in the double doors of
glass and wood. About six, we all met at the
racket-court, whose high wall by that time cast
a sufficient shadow. A couple of four-handed
games (the doctor was grown too stout to play)
left us streaming at every pore, and marking at
each step a damp foot-print through our white
canvas shoes on the pavement. Then the deli-
cious plunge in the swimming-bath in the judge's
garden! the one moment of freshness looked
forward to throughout the exhausting day. A
cheroot and an iced drink, as we lay fanned
by the servants on long chairs at the top of The
Mount—and presently, almost in a minute, the
sun had once more hidden his malignant face, and
the blinding glare of day gave place to the stifling
stillness of night.

Our house entertained on two evenings a week
and we usually dined out two other evenings, with
whist afterwards, and a modest pool at loo on
Saturday nights to afford vent to the doctor's Irish
energies. Sometimes we passed a domestic edict
not to dine till the thermometer fell to ninety-five
degrees, and waited till past nine o'clock without

seeing the mercury sink to that point. But the life was full of compensations. In the first place, an Englishman enjoys capital health in the hot weather, if still young and not afraid of exercise, and with plenty of work. I was living, moreover, with perhaps the most charming and accomplished man in the Service. Ayliffe's resources of companionship were inexhaustible. His unfailing cheerfulness and sweet courtesy of manner were in themselves sufficiently pleasant. But it was rather his quick and genuine sympathy with one's own small efforts and interests that endeared him in daily life. One somehow felt, also, in the presence of a reserve of force.

His many-coloured but pithy talk made the breakfast cheroot a delightful episode in the long hot day. After dinner, when we were alone and not reading or playing chess, we had our cane chairs taken up to the flat roof. There, in the starlight, he would pour forth those stores of incisive observation which have since earned for him a foremost place among Indian Governors and thinkers of our day. On one evening he was the experienced and sagacious administrator, full of the problems of Indian rule. On another, he was the philosopher sitting reflective on the river-bank, and watching with calm but friendly eyes the stream of ancient races and religions as it flowed past.

The story of the Missionary's new peasant settlement interested Ayliffe, and led to an intimacy between the two men. Indeed, the character of 'Trafalgar' Douglas appealed alike to the practical and the speculative side of Ayliffe's nature. The Old Missionary had reached a serene region beyond the perturbations of dogma. We were to find, too, during that hot weather, that his was a calm of soul which no earthly agitation could ruffle—neither the frustration of long-cherished hopes, nor the bitterness of desertion, nor sharp physical pain. For, as the scorching end of April melted into a fiery May, a great calamity befell our aged friend. The glare and hot winds which he faced while portioning out the new village lands must have hastened the failure of eyesight that had been going on for several years. The first day I looked in at his cottage after his return, I found him at his library table, the manuscript of his beloved dictionary spread before him, and his hand resting on the head of his little daughter who was sitting on a low stool by his side.

'It all seems very faint to me,' he said, with an air of pained perplexity; 'can the ink have faded so soon?'

I glanced at the written slips, neatly pasted by the zealous girlish fingers on the sheets of yellow paper. They read as clear as before. The little daughter looked up wistfully at me for a moment, then threw her arms round her father's neck, convulsively kissing his dimmed eyes, and choking with pent-up sobs.

Our good doctor attended him with an anxious kindness that tried, perhaps not altogether in vain, to make up for his lack of ophthalmic science. He told us from the first, however, that, so far as he understood the case, it was a hopeless one — atrophy of the nerves of vision. The judge, on the pretext of a rather stubborn ear-ache caught while sleeping close under the punka, sent for a specialist from Calcutta. The famous surgeon, after doing what was needful for Ayliffe, made a careful examination of the Missionary's eyes. His

report confirmed our worst fears. By that time
Mr. Douglas could only distinguish day from night,
or a bright moving flame, and the professor informed us that no change for the better must be
hoped for. Next morning Ayliffe gently told the
truth to the old man.

In the afternoon I went to sit with our stricken
friend. A dust storm, bringing its torrents of rain,
had cooled the air, but the sun had broken out
again with an insufferable radiance. The Old
Missionary was sitting as before at his table,
which, however, had been drawn close to the
window. One of his hands played in his little
girl's hair, with the other he turned from time
to time the written sheets before him, which he
was never again to see. But on his face rested
a perfect serenity, and his eyes, in which no outward change could be discerned, turned to me with
their old beam of benevolent welcome. As I looked
at him there, surrounded by the great unfinished
work of his life, the work which no man but himself could complete, and from which he was now
shut out for ever, I felt as if any commonplace of
consolation that I could offer would strangle me

in the utterance. The double windows, strangely enough on such a glaring afternoon, had been thrown wide open. I sat for some moments in silence with a heart too full for speech, while he looked mildly out into the intolerable sunshine.

I could only press his hand and stammer some words of deepest sorrow.

'Ah, my dear young friend,' he said with a gentle smile, 'you do not know how much remains to me. I thank my merciful Maker,' he continued, unconsciously raising his sightless eyes to heaven, 'since He has been pleased to hide from me the face of man, and all His lesser creatures, that He has graciously left me His first work of creation, His beautiful gift of light.'

We soon found that this was no momentary exaltation of the mind, but a fixed and calm content. At first we hoped that, with the willing help of Ayton the assistant magistrate (and a Boden Scholar, as I have mentioned, in his Oxford days), the dictionary might go on. Indeed, Ayliffe had a few sheets put in type in Calcutta. On their arrival it was pathetic to see the delight with which the venerable scholar passed his finger-tips across their smooth surface, and then across the rumpled coarse pages of yellow country paper on which the slips of the separate words were pasted. But a fort-night of disappointing effort made it clear that their revision involved a knowledge of the hill-language which the Old Missionary alone possessed. It was a labour altogether beyond the rare hours of leisure which the daily grinding at the official mill-stones allowed to any of us. The Missionary was the first to come to this conclusion, and he begged Ayliffe to go to no further expense in printing.

Then, for a time, we tried to avoid all reference to the matter. But evening after evening we found the blind white-haired scholar at his writing-table, in the fierce glare of the sinking sun, with his long silky fingers travelling alternately over the smooth proof-sheets and the uneven yellow manuscript.

By degrees he made it easy for his friends to talk on the subject. He had peacefully accepted the fact that the finishing of his beloved work was not for him in this world. But he seemed to look on its completion as merely delayed. He never suggested any means for carrying it out, although every now and then there came to the surface a still expectation and quiet trust that the work would be done. One evening he said with a smile: 'After all, I have but ploughed up a new field, and put the seed in the furrows. When the harvest is ready, the Lord will send the reaper into the harvest.'

As Ayliffe and I rode home afterwards, I happened to comment on this curious confidence in a fruition which now seemed so hopeless.

'Leave Now,' Ayliffe quietly answered—

'Leave Now for dogs and apes,
Man has For-ever.'

'I wonder,' I went on, 'if that clever young Brahman whom I heard preaching in the forest will be of any use. I hear he is coming in from the new village to headquarters, to help the Missionary in his current duties.'

'If the Brahman has fibre in him,' replied Ayliffe, 'he may be the prop of this man's old age. Yet who knows? A youth who starts life with such a wrench away from the order of things around him as is implied by conversion, may have strange oscillations before he reaches true equilibrium or poise. He will help no doubt in the school and

religious services, and in giving out medicines to
the sick. But a task like the dictionary is not
to be accomplished by any impulse of emotion:
only by long and steadfast labour.'

I am afraid that the sympathy which we felt for
the venerable scholar, on the break-down of his
magnum opus when so near completion, has somewhat obscured in this narrative the daily routine
of his life. It was not the tradition of the Service
in Lower Bengal to take too vivid an interest in
details of mission work. A friendly subscription
which compromised no one, and a few kindly
words when presiding at the annual distribution of
prizes in the mission school, represented our connexion with proselytizing enterprise. The judge,
as the senior civilian, read prayers officially in the
Circuit House on Sunday afternoons: to have
attended the mission church would have struck us
as an odd, and indeed almost as an irregular pro-
ceeding. But the things of which we knew so little
still formed, as they had formed for forty years,
the staple work of the Old Missionary's day.

In the early morning his daughter led him round
the dilapidated fish-pond to the little chapel on the

opposite side; and there the white head, erect
above the desk, repeated from memory the familiar
Morning Prayers in Bengali to a small gathering
of the mission catechists, a few women, and some of
the school children. From the chapel he went
direct to the adjoining school-house. The pupils,
of whom the majority were non-Christians, had
already assembled, a hundred and thirty strong, in
three long rooms opening one into the other.
When Mr. Douglas stood up at his table they all
joined in a Bengali hymn, followed by a short
prayer from him and a chapter of the Gospels. The
secular work of the day then began. Mr. Douglas
had always aimed, not at ambitious standards of
instruction, but to give a really useful training
to his people, and to make his schools independent of outside aid. Children of every faith
were welcome: the clever ones rose to be pupil-
teachers; and the best of these were in due time
drafted into a normal class, in which they went
through a practical course as schoolmasters.

In this way he obtained a highly qualified staff
for his own central school. He was also enabled
to send out a constant stream of men on whose

moral character and intellectual ability he could
thoroughly rely, to about thirty village schools
which he had set up among the Christian population throughout the District and in the hill-
country. The system was self-supporting. The
fees in the central school, together with the Government grant, more than defrayed its expenses.
The elders of the outlying Christian villages, in
which a teacher had been established, levied
a monthly dole in money and rice for his main-
tenance. The surplus fees from the central station
school supplemented these allowances in the
poorer hamlets.

The Old Missionary's custom was to plant out
a teacher—who was usually although not always
a catechist as well—in a backward tract, and to
maintain him until he gathered together a group
of pupils, often under no better shelter than
a spreading banian-tree. By degrees the villagers
began to take a pride in watching their children
being taught, set up a mat hut for a school-house,
and provided for the subsistence of the master.
The Missionary then withdrew his grant, and
applied the money to planting out a new school

elsewhere. He held that education should not be expected to pay its way, at starting, among people who have never known its value, and that this was a case in which the supply must create the demand. I believe that some such words of his, in a conversation which he held a quarter of a century before with the Governor-General on his Excellency's progress through the District, were the origin of Lord Auckland's similar schools for backward tracts.

Notwithstanding his blindness, the venerable instructor still gave two hours in the early morning to his training class of teachers, each youth in which was to him not only a chosen pupil but a beloved young friend. He also kept what seemed, for so gentle a nature, a marvellously firm hand on the general discipline. Indeed, under his sanction, the head-master used the rod with a freedom unknown in the neighbouring Government school.

One morning, as he paced slowly round the shaded margin of the fish-pond for a little exercise, leaning on my arm, with the hum from his school-house filling the still air, I asked why he laid so much stress on teaching, as compared with the preaching which formed the popular idea of a missionary's work.

'I hope,' he said, quietly, 'that while I do the one I have not left the other undone. In the days of my strength I spoke daily to the people, and now the catechists strive faithfully with them in the bazaars and villages. But I have never forgotten John Lawrence's parting words to me when he passed through Calcutta on sick-leave, in 1840: " The only way that will bring the natives to truer and more enlightened ideas is the gradual progress of education. The attempts to change the faith of the adult population have hitherto failed, and will, I am afraid, continue to fail." '

'But,' I interposed, 'is not our State education doing the needed work on a far larger scale?'

'I greatly fear,' he replied, 'that it is not. Your State education is producing a revolt against three principles which, although they were pushed too far in ancient India, represent the deepest wants of human nature — the principle of discipline, the principle of religion, the principle of contentment. The old indigenous schools carried punishment to the verge of torture. Your Government schools pride themselves in having almost done away with the rod, and in due time you will have on your hands a race of young men who have grown up without discipline. The indigenous schools made the native religions too much the staple of instruction; opening the day's work by chanting a long invocation to the Sun or some other deity, while each boy began his exercise by writing the name of a divinity at the top. Your Government schools take credit for abstaining from religious teaching of any sort, and in due time you will have on your hands a race of young men who have grown up in the public non-recognition of a God. The indigenous schools educated the working and trading classes for the natural business of their lives. Your Government schools spur on every clever small boy with scholarships and money allowances, to try to get into a bigger school, and so through many bigger schools, with the stimulus of bigger scholarships, to a University degree. In due time you will have on your hands an overgrown clerkly generation, whom you have trained in their youth to depend on Government allowances and to look to Government service, but whose adult ambitions not all the offices of the Government would satisfy. What are you to do with this great clever class, forced up under a foreign system, without discipline, without contentment, and without a God?'

The old man had disengaged his arm from mine and was standing motionless, erect, with his sightless eyes looking forth from their deep sockets into space. At that moment it flashed upon me what 'Trafalgar' Douglas must once have been. Twenty years afterwards, when we expanded Indian education on a more national basis, I remembered his words.

'The day will come,' he went on, as in a reverie, 'when your State educators will be face to face with the results. They will be forced back on the old indigenous schools as the sure foundation of public instruction in India. They will find out that races who for ages have borne a heavy yoke throughout life, cannot be trained up without discipline in their youth. They will also discover that the end of national education is not to create

one vast clerkly class, but to fit all classes for
their natural work.   You will then, I suppose,
set up technical schools, to do in some manner
what the old native system of the hedge-school
and the hereditary handicraft did in perhaps an ex-
cessive measure.   The Government will discern the
danger of millions of men growing up in a dis-
credited faith, and it will piece together a moral
text-book to take the place of a God.   I shall
not see that day, I know not how its difficulties
will be met, nor how the great changes which it
must bring may affect our missionary schools.
But night and morning I pray that wisdom may
be given to our rulers to know the times and the
seasons, and to do righteousness to this wandering
people.'

After an eloquent outburst of this kind—and
such outbursts became more frequent as his blindness more and more pent up his nature within
itself—the old man would have a period of
profound calm.   On that particular morning, as
it was the festival of a Hindu goddess and the
Courts were closed, I went in with him to his
dispensary—a little room in his bungalow where

he daily prescribed to the sick at the close of
his school work.   I believe that at one time the
people flocked in numbers to him, and that he even
conducted surgical operations.   But the growing
popularity of the station hospital, supported by
local subscriptions and a Government grant, had
for several years made its wards the centre of
medical relief.   Of the score of very poor women
and children who sat weariedly on the floor of
the Missionary's veranda, only two or three were
new cases.   Most of the others had come with
bottles to be refilled with fever mixture for their
sick folk at home.   The aged practitioner was
very slow and gentle with them, and, notwithstanding his blindness, managed to get a clear
knowledge of each applicant's needs.   A native
compounder made up the prescriptions under his
orders, or replenished the phials and ointment
boxes from big blue bottles and delf jars.   When
the last of his patients had departed, the old
man sat silent for some time.

'I find,' he at length said with a sigh, 'that
my ministrations are not so acceptable as they
once were.   At first, when prescribing medicine,

I offered up in each case a short prayer, in which
the patient joined. This gave great confidence
in the remedies. Before coming back to India
to start doctoring, I held commune with Edward
Irving, and for years I used the Benediction
of Oil and the beautiful order for Anointing
the Sick in the liturgy of the Catholic Apostolic
Church. But I found that the sorcerers in the
hill-country and the old native practitioners of
the border employed somewhat similar ceremonies,
especially in the application of oil. Or rather,
the people did not distinguish between their
incantations and my prayers. If I lost a man
from fever, the widow would bitterly complain that
her husband had died because I had only spoken
words, instead of administering the quinine-powder
wrapped up in a paper with the prayer written
on it.

'When the hill sorcerers asked me for my
secrets, and I gave them a few common remedies,
they thanked me politely. But they went away
and told the villagers that I was very deep, as
I kept to myself the spells, without which the
drugs were merely dead earths. The old Hindu

practitioners of the border country were worse.
For they said that, if they had as good medicines
as mine, their gods would never let their sick
people die at all. So that whenever a man
recovered, the Christian drugs got the credit;
and whenever a man died, the Christian God was
reviled. I could not go on with prayers which
to the hearers were only a more cunning magic.
It would not have been honest. But since I gave
them up, the people have not had the same confidence in my practice, and go to the Government
hospital instead. They say that the medicines
there are administered by order of the Queen,
and so do not require divine aid or spells of
any sort.'

'I can well understand these notions among
the hill-people,' I remarked; 'but surely your
Christian converts know better.'

'Christian converts,' he answered sadly, 'remain,
like other people, pretty much what their early
training has made them. Indeed, some of the
catechists are anxious to again use the prayers
when giving medicine. It so happens that the
very first Christian hymn composed in the Bengali

language was a sick-bed supplication. Only yesterday the Brahman preacher, whom you saw in our
cold-weather encampment, was urging me as their
spokesman in this matter. He is a godly youth,
and but for the work of the new village I had
hoped to send him to Calcutta to be ordained
priest on this coming Trinity Sunday. He has
held deacon's orders for two years. I pointed
out to him that our Anglican liturgy does not
provide for the use of prayers in the administration
of medicine. He respectfully pleaded the precept
of St. James, and I refrained from further speech,
lest I should be a disturber of his faith. His
mind is working in many directions, and in my
weakness I can only trust the end to God.'

Just then we heard a light step in the veranda,
and his little daughter ran round from another
room, saying, with a laugh, 'Have you forgotten
my lessons to-day, dear papa? I am quite ready.'
The old man's face lost its look of care in a moment
as he took her hand in his, and we went into the
library.

Only a short time remained till their breakfast—
the Missionary kept earlier hours than the rest

of the station, finishing his long morning work
by nine in the cold weather, and its still more
numerous duties in the summer months by ten.
The child sat down on a low seat at her father's
knee, and gravely went through her tasks. She
first repeated a psalm in the vigorous Scotch
metrical version, which she had committed to
memory. Then she did her geography, pointing
out the towns of Europe on a map. Her sweet
gratitude and quick tact made the old man feel,
notwithstanding his blindness, that he was taking
an effective part in the proceedings. He listened
with pride as she read out her chapter of history,
asking her from time to time to spell the more
difficult words. Before doing so she would
solemnly each time place the book on his knees,
face downwards, so that she could not see the
page. At the end he questioned her on the
whole lessons of the day. The anxious child had
learned everything so perfectly that her blind
preceptor was not allowed for a moment to feel
his infirmity a hindrance in examining her in
books which he could not see.

Unlike most elderly people in India, the Missionary

took no afternoon sleep. As long as his sight
lasted, he devoted that pause in the tropical day
to his dictionary. Now that this work had been
withdrawn from him, he calmly rearranged his
hours to the new conditions imposed.

Instead of taking the current work of the
mission after breakfast, as his practice had been,
he gave the forenoon to his daughter, telling her
old stories of the Solway and Scottish border,
while she sat beside him and sewed; or listening
to her reading aloud whatever girlish book she
was engaged on; and occasionally dictating to
her letters for his friends. It was a very little
hand that slowly traced those epistles, in which
the mild benevolence and experience of age contrasted quaintly with the large unformed writing
of childhood. After a two o'clock dinner he made
his daughter retire to rest, and the young Brahman
preacher came to him with the reports from the
outlying schools and Christian hamlets, and all
the miscellaneous work of the mission.

Much of the old man's business consisted in
settling disputes of the Christian villagers, and
the veranda gradually filled with the litigants

and their witnesses as the afternoon wore on.
Frequently, too, the headmen of one of the non-
Christian hill tribes would arrive in the mission
enclosure to seek his advice, or to ask him to
decide their differences. Groups of them might be
seen smoking patiently under his mango-trees, or
filling their pitchers at his lotus-covered fish-pond,
which they had named rather prettily in their
hill-language, 'The Waters of Reconciliation.' The
calamity lately fallen upon him increased rather
than lessened this branch of his work. His age
and blindness seemed to have given an additional
sanctity to his decisions.

The circumstance, also, that his doors now stood
wide open all afternoon in spite of the outside
glare, enabled the whole body of onlookers and
petitioners to watch each successive case till their
own turn came. It was indeed a striking sight,
as I witnessed it late one afternoon. The tall
venerable figure, with its white hair and the deep-
set eyes that looked forth into the brightness with
the glance of a grand old eagle, sat just inside the
open door, and listened with an immoveable face to
the loud disputants in the veranda. His very slow-

ness and silence, which had grown painfully on him since his loss of sight, appeared to make the people attach greater weight to every word which at length came reluctantly from his lips. Worried as we officials were by petty cases dragged upwards from one tribunal to another, I could not help telling him when his litigants had gone, that the Missionary's Court was the only judgement-seat in the district from which there seemed to be no appeal.

Having settled their disputes, he went back to the chair at his writing-table, on which lay the specimen proof-sheets and the coarse yellow manuscript of his dictionary—the usual position in which I found him when his day's work was done. We had by this time persuaded him to occasionally take a drive in the evening—a concession which he only made to his daughter's health, and because she firmly refused to come without him. As there was no barouche nor any feminine vehicle in the station, and my Australian Stanhope had the only seat wide enough for three persons, Ayliffe would sometimes put his fine stud-breds into it, and spin them a swift dozen

miles through the cooling air. He was, however,
much more missed in the racket-court than myself, so it usually fell to me to take the father and
child for their evening drive. The old man sat
silent and sightless, but I think quite happy, his
hat off, and his white hair blown about by our
rapid motion, listening to his little daughter as
she chattered about my horses, now old friends
of hers, or discoursed on the small incidents of
her isolated life. It was funny to hear her, in
prim mission-house fashion, always speak of the
natives quite kindly as ' the heathen.'

She had just made acquaintance with *Pilgrim's
Progress*, the assistant magistrate having given her
the beautiful Edinburgh edition, with David Scott's
illustrations, on her tenth birthday. Its forty marvellous designs were all realities to her. We used
to be on the look-out for the various characters
as we whirled along the road. One evening we
met Timorous and Mistrust—they were a couple
of post-runners with jingling bells at the end of
their bamboo staves—fleeing from the lions. On
another, we were quite sure that we saw Simple,
Sloth, and Presumption (three fat grain merchants)

encamped for the hot-weather night under a tree.
Her father was always valorous Christian, and
a certain bazaar of sweetmeat-sellers and bright
printed calicos was Vanity Fair. The hillock in
the judge's garden became the top of the Delectable Mountains, from which she would gaze to
the western hills: half persuaded that amid their
heights and buttresses standing out in the brief
glory of the sunset, she might discern, if she had
but the Shepherds' perspective glass, the gates of
the Celestial City. The only thing wanting to her
father's happiness on these drives was the sound
of the evening bell which the young Brahman had
presented to the mission church. When at home
the venerable pastor, often too fatigued to walk
across to the vesper service, used to sit in his
veranda and listen to the soft tinkle in the belfry
with a look of rapt calm, as if repeating the Nunc
Dimittis in his heart.

I found by degrees, however, that the Brahman
preacher had become to the old man a subject of
anxious thought. Whether it was the result of the
youth's independent position when in charge of
the new village, or of his studies for priestly

H

ordination, or merely the natural development of an earnest young mind, the Brahman had ceased to be the trusting disciple, and was working out conclusions for himself. Mr. Douglas, like most men born in a Scottish episcopal family, had started life with traditions which we should now briefly label as High Church. On his return to Scotland in 1828 to qualify himself as a medical missionary, his views had taken a mystical turn, under the spell of the apocalyptic eloquence with which Edward Irving thrilled for a moment the University youth in the northern capital.

A third of a century of solitary mission work since then had sobered his opinions. As already mentioned, his doctrinal beliefs were softened down into a great daily desire to do good for his people. The young postulant for priest's orders began to find many things wanting in the theology of his old master. I subsequently heard that the Brahman deacon, having now the practical conduct of the mission chapel, had protested against the shortened services which the Old Missionary thought were as much as the people could bear. He also complained of the omission of the Athanasian Creed on the appointed feasts of the Church.

It appears that on Whitsunday he remonstrated about that omission so earnestly with Mr. Douglas as almost to forget his habitual respect. Several of the catechists afterwards called at the mission-house to urge the same view on their pastor. A number of lesser differences, indeed, would seem to have concentrated themselves on this point. The stout-hearted old Scotchman, notwithstanding his sightless eyes and feeble limbs, refused to yield to the pressure.

Revival meetings were held by the dissentients during the Ember days of the following week. One youthful enthusiast went so far as to publicly offer up a prayer that the old man might be brought to a knowledge of the truth. As the mission had been maintained by Mr. Douglas without any definite connexion with either of the great Church societies in Calcutta, there was practically no superior authority to whom to appeal. Something like a schism was threatened. The Old Missionary said not a word to us about his new troubles, and the religious perturbations of native

Christians were little likely to reach our ears. But we could see that a sadness, deeper than the sorrow of blindness, had settled on his face.

It was the custom of Ayton, the assistant magistrate, to spend Sunday morning before breakfast with the venerable scholar, chatting about the linguistic studies to which that young officer then devoted his leisure. The little girl was absent during those hours, keeping quiet the baby-class in the Sunday school with picture stories from the Bible. In these morning talks with Ayton the old man's love of learning would reassert itself. He seemed for the moment to forget his infirmity and whatever other distresses lay hidden in his heart. One topic on which he delighted to descant was the deeply religious and benevolent character of ancient Indian literature. Ayton humoured this vein, and used to turn into English metre any striking passage that he came across in his Sanskrit reading during the week. On the Sunday after the events mentioned in the last paragraph he had brought a few chance verses of the sort, and was just beginning to read them, when I happened to look in. 'They don't come together,'

he was saying to Mr. Douglas, 'and I fear you
will find them a poor paraphrase rather than
a translation. But the mingled feeling of transi-
toriness and trust is characteristic.'

A SANSKRIT PSALM OF LIFE.

Like driftwood on the sea's wild breast,
  We meet and cling with fond endeavour
A moment on the same wave's crest;
  The wave divides, we part for ever.

We have no lasting resting here,
  To-day's best friend is dead to-morrow:
We only learn to hold things dear,
  To pierce our hearts with future sorrow.

Be not too careful for the morn,
  God will thy daily bread bestow:
The same eve that the babe is born,
  The mother's breast begins to flow.

Will He who robes the swan in white,
  Who dyes the parrot's bright green hue,
Who paints the peacock's glancing light,
  Will He less kindly deal with you?

As he was commencing the next verse, an unexpected interruption broke in on these scholarly
nugae. A step hurried over from the chapel.

Ayton and I were sitting out in the veranda on
the other side of the house, so that we could not
see the new-comer, nor he us. The Missionary sat
between us in his customary chair, but just within
the door of the room, and the young Brahman
(for it was he), on entering, must have thought
Mr. Douglas was alone.   The deacon walked
quickly across the room, raised the old man's
hand to his lips, and then, with a haste which
perhaps may have been designed to preclude reflection, burst out in agitated words:—

'My master, my dear master! I have a message
to thee. "Whosoever will be saved, before all
things it is necessary that he hold the Catholic
Faith.   Which Faith, except every one do keep
whole and undefiled, without doubt he shall
perish everlastingly." Forgive me, my father,'
he went on, in a voice quivering from the religious excitements of the week, and his intense
Indian nature now strung up to the verge of
weeping, 'but the words have been in my heart
day and night, and I have striven not to utter
them.   And on my knees this Trinity Sunday
morning I could not hear the sound of my own

prayers by reason of a terrible ringing in my ears, "without doubt he shall perish everlastingly, he shall perish everlastingly."'

A dead silence followed. The young Brahman, still unconscious of any presence except that of his blind master, seemed to have exhausted his powers of utterance. At length the Old Missionary said, very gently:—

'My son, let us pray together.'

It is not for me to repeat that tender and pathetic outpouring of a well-nigh broken heart, intended alone for its Maker in heaven, and for the wandering disciple on earth. At its close, the aged man remained kneeling for some time. Then, after another long pause, he reseated himself in his chair, and reasoned calmly with his pupil. We could not help overhearing what took place. The young Brahman gradually grew excited again, and in the end declared that the people were being starved of the truth.

We gathered, from his high-pitched remonstrances, that he and the native catechists had worked themselves, by revival meetings, into one of those Eastern religious enthusiasms which

drove forth Patriarchs of Alexandria and Con-
stantinople into exile, and which, but for the
firm British rule, would every year redden the
streets of Agra with Hindu or Muhammadan
blood. It had never occurred to us that any
similar wave of religious feeling could surge over
a quiet little community of Christian converts.
The truth seems to be that the younger of the
catechists had for some time desired a warmer
ritual and a more tropical form of faith than the
calm theology of their aged pastor.

A High Church young parson of the Society
for the Propagation of the Gospel, who acted
for the Old Missionary during an illness in the
previous autumn, unconsciously sowed the seeds
of discord. The fervour of the Brahman deacon
merely hastened a crisis which had become in-
evitable in the spiritual life of the mission. One
of the deep chagrins of the Old Missionary, which
he buried out of sight from us, was this feeling
that the most earnest of his people were silently
arraying themselves against him. Amid the religious excitements of the Whitsun week, with its
Ember days, the mission had fairly got out of

hand. At the last revival meeting the catechists resolved, among other things, to insist on the Athanasian Creed being read on the following Trinity Sunday, and deputed the deacon to report their ultimatum.

'So long as I live,' replied the Old Missionary slowly, and with a solemn emphasis on each word, 'the church in which I have preached Christ's message of mercy shall never be profaned by man's dogma of damnation.'

'My father, my father,' the young Brahman answered, almost breaking into sobs, 'do not speak so. For unless you consent to have the full Trinity service, as laid down in the Prayer Book, we have bound ourselves not to enter the chapel.'

'God's will be done,' said the old man sadly, but firmly.

In another minute the deacon had left the room, and we listeners in the veranda, not knowing what consolation to offer, departed in silence to our homes.

Indeed, I had at that time a trouble of my own, which might have inclined me to seek counsel

rather than to tender it. Scarcely eight weeks
had passed since I returned to the judge's house,
after the Easter riot at the silk Factory. During
the last three of them a cloud had come over
my relations with Ayliffe. It is not needful, after
this lapse of time, to apportion the blame. I
suspect, on looking back, that we were both
right, and both too keen.

Having been made a judge *malgré lui*, Ayliffe
set himself not the less strictly and conscientiously
to discharge the duties of his office. The sub-
ordinate native magistrates found an exactitude
enforced from them in their judicial work to
which they had never been accustomed. Some
of them were men of the dignified old type, and
their unacquaintance with English made it difficult
for them to master the hard-and-fast chapters of
the new Penal and Procedure Codes. Their sentences were now constantly reversed on appeal
to the judge owing to flaws in the proceedings,
and notorious offenders got off.

My difficulties, as the officer responsible for
keeping down crime in the District, were increased
by the circumstance that the Bengal police had

also been reorganized by law on an entirely fresh basis. The system was full of novelties both to officers and men, and they found their efforts checkmated by technicalities which they imperfectly understood. Two fraternities of gang-robbers, whom we had tracked down with much difficulty, escaped on their trial before Ayliffe as sessions judge. A sense of discouragement began to pervade the whole executive of the District.

The native magistrates came to me with their grievances; the English superintendent of police less discreetly lamented his wrongs to a friend at the seat of Government. Even Ayton, the assistant magistrate, who had the law at his finger-ends, felt it his duty to urge on me the detriment which was being done to the peace and order of the District. ' It is very well,' he said, ' for the legislature to launch forth new Codes. But unless it can give new men to administer them, or until the old native magistrates have time to master them, a judge defeats the purposes of justice by treating irregularities of procedure as fatal flaws in a case.'

Living as Ayliffe and I were on the most

intimate terms, under the same roof, it was
scarcely possible that we should avoid this subject. I pressed for the allowances which might
fairly be granted to our half-instructed subordin-
ates during a transition stage. He alleged the
express provisions of the law. His sweetness of
temper made anything like a quarrel impossible.
But underneath his considerate courtesy of speech
lay an immovable firmness of purpose. We both
felt it growing dangerous to approach a subject
which we knew was on each other's mind. A sense
of separation arose. We kept more to our respective wings of the building during the day, and
our chairs were no longer carried up to the roof
for the old pleasant talks after dinner. I hurried
on the work-people at my own house, and as soon
as a few rooms could be made weather-tight I
moved over.

One result of the change was that I more frequently found a spare half-hour to look in on
the Old Missionary. I thought it right to tell
him that we had overheard what took place
between him and the young Brahman. The
venerable man, on learning that I was become

aware of his hidden trouble, freely opened his heart. But he altogether refused to share in my perhaps too freely expressed indignation at the deacon's ingratitude. Since the schism on Trinity Sunday neither the deacon nor the catechists had entered the chapel.

'You cannot call ingratitude,' he said, 'a line of action that proceeds from a sense of duty. This affliction has fallen not less heavily on the youth than on myself. I trust in God that He will find a way for both of us through the trial. Meanwhile I have been marvellously renewed for the work laid upon me. The older and simpler among the people cleave to me; and I feel a strength not my own for the whole religious services of the week.'

It became clear, however, as the hot weather dragged on its remorseless length, that the old man was overtaxing both mind and body. He had strange fits of lassitude, from which sometimes the only thing that roused him was the tinkle in the belfry calling him and his faithful few to prayer. The other business of the mission seemed to lose interest for him, while this single

duty grew into an absorbing anxiety. A great
unacknowledged fear took possession of him lest
he should find himself one day unable for the
work. The pupil-teacher who read the Psalms
and other parts of the Bengali service which the
blind pastor did not repeat from memory, complained to the Missionary's little daughter of unwonted omissions and transposals in the Liturgy,
which sometimes made it difficult for him to
know when his own parts came in. Her small
anxious face grew paler day by day, and occasionally I fancied that one caught something like a sob
in her voice.

With the pathetic half-perceptions of childhood,
she felt the presence of a trouble which she could not
alleviate, and a growing sense of calamity around
her which she could not understand. For the first
time, too, she seemed to divine the solitude of her
poor little life. All she could do was to suffer in
fear and silence. Even the small distractions of
her lonely existence were one by one curtailed.
Her father was now too wearied before evening
to rouse himself for the slight exertion of a drive.
I learned also, by accident, that the child had

given up bringing her lessons to him in the morning. She seems to have spent the long stifling hours of the day in wistfully waiting on his slightest wishes: always watching, watching, with a child's keen sense of a great, undefined sorrow in the house.

It was in vain that we remonstrated with the venerable pastor against his persisting in duties which were evidently beyond his powers. 'As my day is, so shall my strength be,' was all we could get from him in reply. Indeed it became clear that, if he had not taken on himself the whole religious services of the mission, the revivalists would have left him without any adherents whatever. They had formed a temporary congregation under the eloquent ministrations of the young deacon. The Brahman appeared, however, to hold back rather than lead on the more fervid spirits among the rank and file of converts from the low-castes. I afterwards heard that he rebuked from the pulpit certain of the catechists, who wished to widen the separation and make it permanent by applying for a new English missionary to the Society for the Propagation of the Gospel in

Calcutta. All this, and probably much more, must have been known to our old friend, and explains his intense anxiety to maintain the services and so tide the mission over its time of trial. The chapel bell at morning and evening seemed to have grown dearer to him as the sole remaining symbol of peace.

One forenoon, just before the courts closed for the rest of the flaming day, I received a note from the doctor asking me to look in at the mission-house on my way home. He himself met me in the veranda, and whispered that the painful complaint from which the Missionary suffered the previous year at the end of the rains had broken out again. He did not, however, think the attack more serious than the last one, although the hot weather was very much against him. On entering I found the library turned into a sick-room. The bed on which the patient lay, a common country *charpoy* strung with coarse fibre, had been brought in from his sleeping chamber, and placed in the middle of the floor under the punka. For the first time since his blindness all the double doors and windows were shut up, and it took some moments before my vision accustomed itself to the darkness. The tight-drawn face was flushed and red in its setting of white hair, the lips muttered in high fever, the eyes from time to time moved with a restless brightness which made it difficult to believe they did not see.

One hand twitched ceaselessly at the sheet, the other was clasped by his little daughter who sat on her low cane stool by the bedside. She had arranged the accessories of a sick-room on a small round table within her reach—the phials, and moist sponge, and cool porous earthen pitcher of water. Every few minutes she gently removed the hot handkerchief from her father's forehead, and replaced a newly-wetted one on his brow. The appealing, wearied look that had pained us during the past weeks had gone out of her small face, and she watched every movement of the sufferer with a solemn and silent earnestness which was entirely unconscious of her own anxieties and deep trouble.

'He must have been struggling with illness for some time,' said the doctor, when half an hour afterwards we went back into the veranda.

I

'I suspect, too, that he got touched by the sun this morning as he walked across to the chapel, and so brought matters to a crisis. About seven o'clock a man came running to me in the hospital, crying that the Padre Saheb was in a fit. It appears that on kneeling down, after giving the Benediction at the close of the service, he remained motionless for some time and then fell forward on the pavement. I found him lying there unconscious, with his daughter holding up his head in her arms. The fever, I hope, is chiefly the result of the sun, and should pass off. But his former malady has been doing mischief again.

'The poor old man must have been in great pain for several days without telling any one. I shall camp here for the afternoon, and as soon as my servant brings over my breakfast I hope to persuade the little girl to eat something, and get her off to bed for a couple of hours. It will be time enough to relieve me for my evening round at five o'clock, and you can arrange with the others for the night.'

The division of duties was easily made. Ayliffe took the first watch, and meanwhile sent off a servant to Calcutta to fetch up a block of Wenham ice in a thick new horse-blanket. For, although the railway had brought the capital within eight hours of us by train and relays of horses, ice was still only an occasional luxury in our small station, and local ice-making machines were then scarcely used in India. The assistant magistrate and district superintendent of police shared the night between them, and I came on at daybreak.

The distant jail gong was striking five in the still air, with the first dim pink just tinging the eastern sky, as I walked over to the Old Mission-ary's cottage. But I found the little girl already dressed and sitting on her cane stool watching the sleeper. Ayton told me that she had heard the runners come in with the ice an hour earlier, and at once presented herself to see it chopped up, and to fold it in the handkerchief on her father's forehead. The old man quickly felt the relief, and after a restless night sank into a profound slumber. The doctor called soon after six and, without disturbing the sleeper, gave a good account of his condition. The improve-ment was maintained during the day, and we

I 2

hoped that the attack was a mere touch of the sun, which would run its course and leave the patient none the worse. Our small bachelor community at once fell into the routine of nursing him in watches of four hours, leaving him to his daughter for the afternoon.

But in a day or two the doctor told us that the former complaint had reasserted itself in a dangerous form, and that a small operation would be needful. Before the week was out we were compelled to accept the fact that our old friend was struggling for his life against prostration and pain, and an exhausting fever which he could not shake off. His servant, a hard-working devout old Musalman, who represented in that modest household the joint train of Hindu and Muham- madan domestics in ordinary Anglo-Indian estab- lishments, never quitted the door of the sick-room except to prepare his master's food in the kitchen, or to pray with his face towards Mecca five times each twenty-four hours. Day and night he was ready at the slightest call: always calm, always helpful, always in spotless white garments, and apparently needing no sleep, save what he could snatch sitting on his heels, with a rocking movement, in the veranda.

The poor little girl broke down on the day after the operation, chiefly, I think, owing to the moans which the sufferer unconsciously uttered while in his fever. She was taken over to Ayliffe's house. But she pined there so silently and piteously, that the doctor brought her back to her father, on condition that she should only attend on him during the latter part of the day, when he was at his brightest. He usually rallied in the afternoons, and talked quite cheerfully of the future. The heavy anxiety about the work of the mission, which had pressed on him with a morbid consuming apprehension just before his illness, seemed to have disappeared. Nor from first to last, except during the delirium of the recurring fever, did he utter a complaint, or allow himself to give one outward symptom of pain.

It was only from the doctor that we learned how much he suffered. He would not allow any of us to move him in his bed, lest the mere change of position should extort a groan. And, indeed, his old servant had an almost feminine

tenderness of touch, and a slow gentleness of hand
that made us feel him to be a better nurse than
any of us.

The little girl also rallied, now that she was
restored to her father. The old man and the child
spent the hours of each afternoon together, scarcely
speaking, but quite happy as long as they felt the
clasp of one another's hand. Only towards sunset,
at the hour when the chapel bell had formerly
rung for evening prayer, he became restless and
watchful. Sometimes he would half raise his head
in a listening attitude, and then, having waited in
vain for the beloved sound in the now silent belfry,
the white hair would sink back on the pillow,
while a look of pained perplexity settled on his
face. During the night, when the fever was on
him, he would ask again and again in a weary
tone, ' Why did I not hear the bell? why do they
not ring the bell?'

Meanwhile the news had reached the jungle
country that the Old Missionary lay sick. Groups
of short thick-built hillmen began to encamp on
the outskirts of his orchard. When it became
known that his life was in danger, their women

also arrived. In the early morning we saw them
silently drawing water from the fish-pond; all
through the burning day they sat smoking and
waiting under the trees; the dying embers of their
cooking fires glowed with a dull red throughout
the night. The doctor wanted to send them away,
so as to keep the sick house as clear as possible
of human beings. But the Old Missionary pleaded
for them, and, indeed, the space was large enough
if they would only be quiet. It was marvellous
to see that gathering of hillmen, accustomed to the
incessant chatter of their forest hamlets, stealing
noiselessly about or sitting in silent circles.

One afternoon the headmen of the Christian
clans were allowed to come into the veranda, but
the sight of their blind and prostrate leader and
the presence of unknown Europeans (the doctor
and myself) seemed to take away their powers of
speech. The Old Missionary talked kindly but
feebly to them, while they stood shy and restrained,
almost without a word. The interview threatened
to end in awkward silence, when an aged grey-
haired hill-woman, the mother of one of the
prisoners whose release the Missionary had ob-

tained, pushed through the men and, throwing herself on her knees at the bottom of the bed, kissed
the old man's feet with sobs and blessings.

Next week the hillmen and people from the outlying jungle-hamlets flocked into the station in
such numbers that they had to be removed from
the mission enclosure. The judge gave them leave
to camp at the lower end of his park, where there
was a large tank; and only their headmen were
allowed to come and sit in silence under the
Missionary's trees. The old Musalman servant
went out to them five times a day, at his appointed
prayer-times, to report how his master fared.

I had not met the Brahman deacon since the
rupture between him and the Old Missionary; but
I heard that Ayton, the assistant magistrate, had
spoken to him in such unsparing terms as pre-
vented him from coming near the mission-house.
Their interview was a painful one. The young
Brahman, confident that he was acting under divine
guidance, yet very unhappy about the human
results of his action, sought counsel of Ayton,
as the only one of us who had previously come
much in contact with him or shown him kindness.

Ayton, nerved by the harsh justice of youth, listened in silence until the deacon reached the point in regard to which the schism had actually taken place—the Athanasian Creed. Then he coldly observed:—

'You are an educated man and a University graduate. Before you quarrelled with your bene-factor on such a question, you would have done well to have read your Gibbon.'

'I came to you, sir,' replied the Brahman, 'seeking counsel, and willing to bear reproof; and you refer me to a scoffer.'

'On a man who can act as you have acted,' Ayton sternly answered, 'counsel would be thrown away, and I have no authority to administer reproof. Nor am I aware that Gibbon, in his account of Athanasius, errs in anything unless on the side of a too enthusiastic admiration. But, although I have neither counsel nor reproof for you, I may plainly tell you that your conduct seems to me the basest ingratitude.'

'I have but followed my lights.'

'Followed your lights! Split up a community, and brought sorrow on your benefactor in his

blindness and old age, for the sake of a creed compiled centuries after the death of the man whose
name it bears—a creed passed over in silence by
most of the Christian sects, and by the majority of
our own Church in America and in Ireland. How
can you look around you at the good lives and
patient endurance of millions of your countrymen,
and dare to assert they will perish everlastingly?
You say you have come to me for advice; but
what advice can avail you as long as you are in
mutiny against the man to whom, by every tie
of personal gratitude and constituted authority,
you owe obedience?'

When the Old Missionary grew worse, I heard
that the deacon used to steal into the kitchen (an
outhouse at a little distance from the cottage) after
dark, and tremulously question the old Musalman
servant about his master. In his deep dejection
the youth even went to Ayton's pandit, a fine old
Brahman of the straitest sect of Hinduism; but
with whom the convert now felt a new bond from
their common anxiety about their sick friend.
Each morning the pandit, arrayed in delicate
white muslin, came to make his salaam at the

door of his venerable fellow-student; and sometimes he was allowed a short talk with our patient
in the afternoon. He kept the deacon informed
of what was going on inside the cottage, with
the quiet urbanity due to his own sacred character
as a pandit of high caste, but without any pretence
of sympathy for the convert.

One evening the unfortunate young man was
tempted in his desolation to try to get within the
barrier of politeness which the courteous native
scholar habitually interposed. He poured forth the
successive episodes of the inward struggle which
made up the story of his short life; a struggle which
had cut him off from all he held dearest in boy-
hood, and which now separated him from the sorely
stricken master whom he reverenced and loved.

'Tell me, Pandit,' he concluded, 'you who have
lived long, and who seem to have attained to so
perfect a peace, what is my duty? How shall
I find rest?'

'Poor youth,' replied the Pandit, with calm
compassion, 'what rest can there be for one who
was born a Brahman and has fallen away from
Brahmanhood? During thousands of years your

Brahman fathers in each generation have sought after divine knowledge, and the same burden was laid upon you by your birth. In your boyish impatience you listened to teachers who thought they could suddenly impart to you the truth—the truth which you are compelled by your Brahman's nature to search out for yourself as long as you shall live.'

'But, sir, you forget that the truth which they gave me was given not of themselves, but was revealed by God.'

'A revealed religion,' continued the Brahman impassively, 'is a short cut to a false sense of certainty in regard to divine things. It is useful for the lower castes, whose lives of toil do not leave them leisure for severe thought. Therefore our fathers provided incarnations for the common people, and so shadowed forth in visible forms the conceptions which they themselves had worked out regarding God. But they never set fetters on religious thought by confining it within the limits of a final revelation, well knowing that, from the first, man has made God in his own image and continues to thus remake Him in each succeeding age. A mind like yours, compelled by

its nature to go on inquiring throughout life
after truth, yet shut up within the prison-walls
of an ancient and a final revelation, can neither
dwell in peace with its fellow-captives nor find
peace for itself. In such a religion a Brahman,
if he is to obtain rest, must stifle his Brahman's
spirit of inquiry by eating beef, and drinking beer,
and by absorbing himself, as the European gentlemen do, in worldly anxieties and successes.'

' Sir,' interposed the deacon reverently, ' my
peace of mind in the future I leave to God; but
what is my present duty ? '

' You have been born a Brahman, and, although
fallen, you cannot divest yourself of your birth.
Your duty is not to disgrace it. Your new religion allows you, a young man, to set up your
immature ideas of divine things against the ripe
knowledge of your teacher, and leads you to
desert him in his blindness and old age. In such
a religion I can find for you no rule of conduct.
But as a Brahman you are bound by the first
rule of your Brahmanhood to obey your spiritual
guide. You have chosen your spiritual guide for
yourself. Submit yourself to him.'

Meanwhile the rains were due in our District in ten days, and if our old friend could only last till the great climatic change, the doctor gave us good hopes of him. A second operation, of a painful although not serious nature, had been found necessary; but the perfect peace of mind of the patient helped him through the crisis. He passed the long hot hours with his hand clasped in his little daughter's, very placid, and apparently without any burden of outward care, except when the silence of the chapel bell at sunset awakened some painful memory. The good Jesuit had journeyed into the station to visit his sick friend, and stayed to take his share of the nursing.

Indeed, what between this kindly priest, and the old Musalman servant, and the little daughter, our turn for attendance now came only every second night, and the strain on the few Europeans in the station passed off. The stream of life flowed feebly in our old friend, yet without perceptible abatement. Each morning, too, the telegrams in the Calcutta newspaper announced stage by stage the approach of the rains, with their majestic cloud-procession northwards across

India, bringing nearer by so many hundred miles a day the promise of relief.

The Jesuit father had his quarters in my half-repaired house, and late one Saturday night, as he was pacing up and down the veranda in meditation, I heard a voice address him in a low appealing tone. It was the unhappy deacon, tempest-tossed with internal conflicts and agonies, who had come to him in the darkness.

'Reverend sir,' he said, in short, agitated sentences, 'take pity on me. I am in great misery. My conscience tells me I am acting right, but my heart accuses me of acting wrong. Oh, help me to the truth! There is no one else to whom I can go. Those with whom I am joined feel no doubts. They reproach me with mine. I come to you as a priest, to tell me what to do.'

'My son,' replied the Jesuit father, 'you cannot come to me as a priest. For you have halted halfway between the darkness of heathendom and the light of the Church. But although you cannot come to me as priest, you may come to me as a friend. And as a friend I earnestly counsel you to seek forgiveness for the wrong you have done.'

'But how can I go against my conscience, and sacrifice to my human affection the appointed order of my Church?'

'Your conscience,' rejoined the Seminarist, 'is in this case only a name for your private judgement. You and your aged teacher have equally applied your private judgements to what you call the appointed order of your Church. The question is whether you will submit your private judgement to his, or set up your private judgement above his. He is your master and your benefactor. Again I say, seek his forgiveness for the wrong you have done.'

No words followed, and the deacon disappeared into the darkness out of which he had emerged. Years afterwards, he told me that he wandered in desolation throughout that night, finding himself unconsciously circling round and round the mission enclosure. The thought took possession of his mind that each of the very different counsellors to whom he had gone had enjoined on him the same course. Obey your superior officer, the assistant magistrate had practically said. Submit yourself to your spiritual guide, repeated the

Brahman sage. Ask forgiveness, commanded the
Jesuit priest. His confidence gave way under the
self-questionings of the slow solemn hours of darkness and solitude. But his duty to those who looked
to him as their leader and guide filled his mind with
an obscurity deeper than that of the night.

Only as the sun rose was his resolve taken.
Worn out, haggard, his cotton clothes dripping
with dew, and stained a muddy red from the
iron clay-stone of which the roads in our District
were made, he went round to each of the
catechists and their chief followers, and summoned
them to the room which they used as a place
of worship. It was Sunday morning, and they
came expecting some new revival excitement.
After an earnest prayer he made a public con-
fession before them. He told them in a few
humble and touching words that he felt he had
wronged his master. Without judging others,
he declared his own resolve to seek forgiveness
of the Old Missionary. Then, commending
himself to their prayers, he left the room amid
a dead silence.

The Old Missionary got his best sleep in the

K

cool of the morning, and on that Sunday he awakened rather later than usual. He had finished his light invalid's breakfast, and was listening to his little daughter reading the ' Let not your heart be troubled ' chapter of St. John's Gospel, when a familiar voice, not heard in the cottage for many days, asked through the heavy venetians, ' May I come in, sir?' In another minute the young deacon was kneeling by his bedside sobbing out his repentance, and covering the wasted silky hands with tears and kisses. ' My son, my dear, dear son,' was all the old man could say.

For some hours he remained in an ecstatic state of joy and peace, until, wearied out by excess of happiness, he sank in the afternoon into a profound slumber. Before he woke it was evening, and the chapel bell, after weeks of silence, was giving out its gentle sound on the other side of the fish-pond. During some moments a smile played over the face of the sleeper. Then, completely awakening, he raised his head on his arm, and listened with a look of beatified repose. The Brahman deacon, who was still by his bedside, kissed his worn hand, and rose to go to the chapel.

'My father,' he said, 'once more give me your forgiveness and blessing.' The old man stretched out both hands on the youth's head, offered up an almost inaudible thanksgiving, and added, 'Let them sing "For ever with the Lord."'

It was one of his favourite hymns, and he had translated it with rare felicity both into the Bengali and the hill language. The highland people thronged the chapel from their camping-ground at the lower end of the judge's park. The catechists and their followers were also there. The schism was at an end. The congregation, for the first time in the history of the mission, overflowed the chapel and stood crowding under the trees between its porch and the lotus-pond.

The deacon's voice, as he read the service, came clear and soft in the still Sabbath evening across the small piece of water. When they raised the hymn, the Old Missionary listened with a rapt look, but at first almost in awe at the unwonted volume of sound, and clasped tighter his little girl's hand. Each cadence rolled slowly forth from the mixed multitude of low-landers and hillmen, to that air in which pathos

mingles so tenderly with triumph. As they came
to the beautiful lines, ' Yet nightly pitch my moving
tent A day's march nearer home,' the old man
suddenly sat up erect, and ejaculated, ' Lord, now
lettest Thou Thy servant depart in peace, according
to Thy word. For mine eyes have seen Thy
salvation.' Then, folding his little daughter, who
was sitting on the edge of the bed, in his long thin
arms, he whispered, ' My darling, my darling!' and
pressed her close to his breast. There was silence
for a minute. Presently the little girl gave a
frightened cry. The Old Missionary was dead.

Next evening we buried him. Amid the cease-
less changes of Anglo-Indian life there is one spot
—only one—that is always quiet. Let a man re-
visit even a large Bengal station after a few years,
and which of the familiar faces remain? He finds
new civilians in the courts, a new uniform on the
parade ground, strange voices at the mess-table,
new assistants in the indigo factories. The ladies
who bowed languidly from their carriages are
bowing languidly elsewhere: as for the groups
of children who played round the band-stand,

one or two tiny graves are all that is left of them
in the station. The Englishman in India has no
home, and he leaves no memory.

In a little station like ours the grave-yard was
very solitary. Of the sleepers beneath the tombs
not one had a friend among the living. Some
of them had fallen with sword in hand, some
had been cut off in the first flush of youthful
promise, some had died full of years and honour.
One fate awaited all. No spring flowers were
ever left on their far-off graves, no tear was ever
dropped, no prayer ever breathed, beside their
resting-place. At the beginning of each cold
season the magistrate entered the walled enclosure with the public works officer to see what
repairs were needful: at the end of the cold season
he inspected it again, to see that the repairs had
been carried out. During the rest of the year
the dead lay alone, through the scorching blaze
of summer and under the drenching deluge of
the rains, alone, unvisited, forgotten.

Yet the solitary place in our small station had
a beauty of its own. In its centre rose an aged
tamarind-tree, which spread out its great arms

and clouds of feathery foliage wide enough to
overshadow all the graves. The oldest sleeper
in that sequestered spot was a little girl. A judge
of the last century lost his only daughter, and,
in the absence of any consecrated plot of ground,
buried her under the tamarind at the foot of his
garden. On its lowest arm the father had put
up a swing for his child. The branch yet faintly
showed the swollen rings where the ropes cut
into the once tender bark. Beneath might be read
the inscription on her tomb: 'Arabella Brooke,
obiit 6 November, 1797.'

Soon another father had to lay his child under
the shade of the tamarind-tree ; and the spot was
decently walled off from the rest of the garden.
Less than seventy years added about thirty English tombstones ; but the graves of little children
still lay thickest. More than one young mother
sleeps there with her baby on her breast. A
headstone, without name or date, to a Lieutenant
killed while leading his detachment against the
hillmen, had been set up by hasty comrades who
passed on before it was ready for the inscription. Beneath another lies a youthful Civilian

THE STATION GRAVE-YARD

who had reached his first station in India only
to die.

They lay so close to us, those lonely dead
people, and yet were so far away! As we chatted
evening after evening in our long chairs on the
top of The Mount, after our swim in the judge's
lake, we could have thrown a pebble among the
tombs. Yet, except for my brief official inspec-
tions to see to the repairs, none of us had ever set
foot within those high walls. One feature of the
place spoke plaintively of the sense of exile and
longing for home: all the graves looked wistfully
towards the West.

Never had the little enclosure witnessed such
a gathering as that which convoyed the Old Missionary to his resting-place. The wild grief of
the hill-people, and the wailing with which the
lowland women rent the preceding night, had
settled down into a sense of loss too deep for
utterance. The bereaved Israel followed their
father and leader in silence, broken only by an
occasional low sobbing, to his grave. The re-
pentant deacon and catechists and the headmen
of the hill Christians carried the coffin. Ayliffe

and I, with the little girl between us, came next.
By a short Will, written with the last rays of
his fading eyesight, her father had appointed us
joint guardians of his child.   The three other
English officials and Father Jerome followed;
then the great stricken multitude.

Nor were the mourners only those of his own
people.   The news had spread with Indian swift-
ness into the hills, and the non-Christian tribesmen
hurried in under their chiefs, forty miles without
a pause for food or water, to do honour to their
White Father and Friend.   The last time that the
clans marched into the District they had come
with weapons in their hands and a line of blazing
hamlets on their track.   Crowds of Musalmans of
all ranks, from the senior native magistrate and
the officiants at the mosque to the shopkeepers
from the closed bazaar, lined the wayside and
salaamed as the coffin passed.   Further off a
group of Hindus and pandits of high caste stood
apart, in respectful silence.   As we reached the
gate of the enclosure, Father Jerome withdrew
from the procession and knelt down by himself
outside the wall.

The little girl stood, weeping noiselessly, between Ayliffe and myself beside the open grave. One small hand trembled in mine, the other clasped Ayliffe's left, while in his right he held the Prayer Book from which he read the burial service. As the final words of consolation melted into silence, and the jungle-villagers began to fill up the grave, the deacon raised in Bengali the hymn which had been so suddenly broken off the previous evening by the summons of death. Again the song of blended tenderness and triumph soared aloft from the multitude of hill-people and men of the plains —its refrain now sounding as a psalm of assured victory—' For ever with the Lord.'

When it ended, Ayliffe said to me softly, 'Come home to me again. The differences between us are over, for I leave immediately to take our little ward to England. He would have wished her to be with us both, during her remaining days here.' The last act of the Old Missionary had been an act of forgiveness and blessing: the first influence of his memory was an influence of reconciliation and peace.

At a sign from Ayliffe the crowd quietly dispersed, leaving us three for a few minutes beside the newly-filled grave.   When at length we turned slowly away, the sun was sinking behind the distant ranges, with two isolated flat-topped hills standing out in front like guardian fortresses on the plain.   It was the sunset-land of brief splendour, towards which the little girl had so often strained her eyes on the wooded height in the judge's garden, when she wished for the Shepherds' perspective glass through which Pilgrim looked from the Delectable Mountains.   She now gazed through her tears on the far-off glory for a moment in silence, and then whispered, ' At last, at last I see the gates of the Celestial City.'